'So, you decided to stand me up, did you?'

Sara recognised Chris Stephens' voice and her mind began ticking over again.

'No more than you deserve,' she snapped back before she could stop herself. 'You didn't exactly make a great effort to welcome me when I first arrived.'

She heard a low, throaty chuckle. 'Something came up; I couldn't get to the airport in time. Can I buy you dinner to make up for it?'

Dear Reader,

This month Caroline Anderson begins a trilogy detailing the loves of three women who work with children and babies at the Audley Memorial Hospital. PLAYING THE JOKER opens with Jo, whose traumatic past she must keep from Alex—a deeply emotional read. Margaret Barker takes us to Bali, while James plans to snare Marnie in SURGEON'S STRATEGY by Drusilla Douglas, and Jenna Reid finds her looks deny her the man she wants in Patricia Robertson's HEART IN JEOPARDY.

Enjoy!

The Editor

Margaret Barker pursued a variety of interesting careers before she became a full-time author. Besides holding a BA degree in French and linguistics, she is a Licentiate of the Royal Academy of Music, a state registered nurse and a qualified teacher. Happily married, she has two sons, a daughter and an increasing number of grandchildren. She lives with her husband in a sixteenth-century thatched house near the sea.

Recent titles by the same author:

HAND IN HAND
FOR LOVE'S SAKE ONLY

ROMANCE IN BALI

BY
MARGARET BARKER

MILLS & BOON LIMITED
ETON HOUSE   18–24 PARADISE ROAD
RICHMOND   SURREY   TW9 1SR

All the characters in this book have no existence outside the imagination of the Author, and have no relation whatsoever to anyone bearing the same name or names. They are not even distantly inspired by any individual known or unknown to the Author, and all the incidents are pure invention.

All Rights Reserved. The text of this publication or any part thereof may not be reproduced or transmitted in any form or by any means, electronic or mechanical, including photocopying, recording, storage in an information retrieval system, or otherwise, without the written permission of the publisher.

This book is sold subject to the condition that it shall not, by way of trade or otherwise, be lent, resold, hired out or otherwise circulated without the prior consent of the publisher in any form of binding or cover other than that in which it is published and without a similar condition including this condition being imposed on the subsequent purchaser.

*First published in Great Britain 1992
by Mills & Boon Limited*

© Margaret Barker 1992

*Australian copyright 1992
Philippine copyright 1992
This edition 1992*

ISBN 0 263 77948 3

*Set in 10 on 12 pt Linotron Times
03-9212-49489*

*Typeset in Great Britain by Centracet, Cambridge
Made and printed in Great Britain*

CHAPTER ONE

As IF by magic, that first heady dive into the sea spirited away her troubles. Sara couldn't remember the last time she'd experienced the sensuously soothing touch of warm sea-water bathing her hot skin. The new white bikini, bought in such a mad rush at C&A in Oxford Street on the very day she had heard the thrilling news that she had been selected for the Bali nursing assignment, wasn't exactly skimpy, but it still gave her more freedom of movement than the ancient, staid swimming costume she'd worn in the London swimming baths over the past few years.

As she struck out through the waves her body felt invigorated; the toll taken by the long, tiring journey from England was paid and forgotten. The distressing fact that there had been no one to meet her at the airport and none of the normal courtesies she had expected when she'd read and re-read the letter of introduction to the Lotus Clinic in Kuta faded into insignificance as she cut through the surf. This was pure escapism, and it was exactly what she needed.

But even as she swam away from the shore her mind registered danger. She had been one of the strongest swimmers at school, swimming at county level before her marriage, and she knew all about the dangers of ignoring the currents of the sea. After her marriage to Mike, she'd had a demanding sister's post to hold down at St Celine's Hospital in London, and her only swimming sessions had consisted of an occasional half-hour at the local baths during her off duty. But she hadn't forgotten her respect for the unpredictable moods of the sea.

And she remembered reading in her guide book to Bali that there was an old myth which said that the goddess of the sea claimed at least one victim each year at Kuta Beach. She shivered in spite of the warmth of the water and promised herself to be careful.

As the shoreline receded she could feel the strong undertow of the salty water; it seemed to be coming at her from all sides with no sense of time or rhythm.

Better turn around, she decided.

She plunged back through the waves, strong arms striking through the perilous current. She had underestimated the opposition; a weaker swimmer would have floundered and come to grief.

As she dragged herself on to the beach she was panting breathlessly. The goddess of the sea was certainly brooding out there somewhere! She resolved not to go so far again. Strong swimmer or not, it made no difference if the sea was in an angry mood.

She lay on the shore at the water's edge, allowing the small waves to lap over her. As she caught her breath, she ran a hand through her long, tangled midbrown hair, feeling the sand that was clinging to her scalp.

Her eyes moved along the shoreline; several yards away a small crowd was gathering. They were looking down at something on the ground. Sara's enquiring nature rose to the surface. Was it one of the giant turtles she'd heard about, or one of the huge fish that swam near the shore?

Her blood ran cold as the crowd parted to allow an inert figure to be carried away up the beach. But, almost immediately, her cool professionalism took over as she leapt to her feet, running as fast as she could towards the crowd. For in that brief second she'd glimpsed a second body on the wet sand, and no one seemed to be caring for this one.

'It's no good, my dear.' A tall, fatherly man, with a North Country English accent, put his hand on her shoulder and tried to stop her moving into the centre of the circle of onlookers. 'The poor guy's had it. He was nearly dead when my friend swam out to bring him back. My friend's a good swimmer, but he took a hammering from the waves. They're taking him to the hospital for a check-up. I'm following on, so I'll get the ambulance to come back and pick this one up. . .'

'But you can't just leave him lying here!'

Sara was incensed as she pushed her way to the middle of the crowd and knelt down beside the motionless form of a young, bearded man. At first glance she decided he was probably in his twenties.

The crowd went quiet as they watched the bikini-clad figure heaving the victim on to his side. Some of them drifted away, not liking what they saw.

A gush of foam-like froth emptied itself on to the sand as Sara worked on the young man. She put her fingers into his mouth, desperate to clear an airway. She felt for his pulse. There wasn't one. The face was congested and livid in colour.

She opened her mouth wide, took a deep breath,

sealed her lips around the nose and mouth and blew gently into his lungs.

From somewhere up above her she heard a deep voice.

'Need any help? I'm a doctor.'

She removed her mouth and for a couple of seconds her eyes made contact with those of the tall stranger towering above her.

'I'm a nursing sister,' she said quickly. 'You can take over when I'm tired.'

Another deep breath and her lips were sealed once more over the victim's nose and mouth. There wasn't a second to be lost. This was no time to stand on protocol. Not when a man's life was at stake. . .if indeed there was any life left in this cold, motionless body.

She was aware that the man who claimed to be a doctor was now squatting beside her on the shore. His linen trousers were soaked with sea-water and sand as he leaned towards her.

'Here, let me take over,' he said after a whole minute had elapsed and no sign of life had appeared.

Sara leaned back on her heels, not unwilling to be relieved of her onerous task.

She watched, her mind only half registering the doctor's actions, her eyes glued to the victim's chest as she willed it to rise.

'Don't give up,' she whispered.

The stranger's eyes narrowed as he took another deep breath. 'I don't intend to,' he muttered.

The remains of the crowd were losing interest and

drifting back to their holiday pursuits. They were writing off the incident as unfortunate.

'Poor chap. . .never stood a chance. . .'

'Must have been mad to swim that far out in this sea. I remember once when I was. . .'

Only the two of them remained, squatting on the sand. And then, just as they were about to give up, Sara gave an excited cry.

'His chest moved!'

The stranger put his fingers on the victim's breastbone, applying pressure with obviously skilled fingers. Relief flooded through Sara. Here was someone who knew exactly what he was doing. She was prepared to believe he was a doctor. Before that, she had neither believed nor cared. He had had the basic skills of First Aid at his fingertips, and that was all that was required. But now that their patient was showing signs of life, it would require skilled medical knowledge and expertise to bring him back from the brink.

The doctor placed the heel of his hand on the lower half of the breastbone and covered this with the heel of his other hand. Then, with arms straight, he rocked forward, pressing down on the lower half of the breastbone.

'I can feel a pulse!' Sara's eyes shone with relief as she faced the doctor.

He pulled himself to a sitting position on the sand, one hand still resting on the patient's chest.

'I think he's going to make it,' he said hoarsely. 'Let's get him to the clinic and make sure.'

'The clinic?' she queried. 'Don't you mean the hospital?'

'I'm in charge at the clinic, so I'll be able to keep an eye on him,' the man explained.

'The Lotus Clinic?'

He gave her a ghost of a smile. 'Fame at last! We've only been opened a few months. Where did you hear about us?'

'I'm Sara Freeman—I'm coming to work for you. You must be. . .'

'Chris Stephens.' He held out a wet, sandy hand and grasped hers in a firm grip. 'Stay here, Sister, while I get on the car phone. We'll need a stretcher and a couple of hefty male nurses.'

Sara sat back on her heels, watching the tall, light brown-haired doctor sprinting across the sand towards the road. With one hand she held on to her patient's wrist, checking the constant pulse. His face was still a deathly colour, but she knew that with the steady, rhythmical breathing that was now in progress, the oxygen would soon diffuse his blood.

She turned to look at the mountainous waves.

'A lucky escape,' she whispered, admonishing the mythical goddess of the sea.

Dr Stephens was returning. She saw him striding across the sand, his wet trousers clinging to the contours of his muscular legs. It was only now, when she had time to think about herself, that she remembered how annoyed she had been with this medical director of the Lotus Clinic as she'd waited in the hot, overcrowded Arrivals area of Ngurah Rai Airport at Denpasar. A whole hour she'd wasted before deciding they had forgotten her and she'd better make it under her own steam to Kuta. As she had paid off the taxi at the

Lotus Clinic she had made a mental note that she would charge the fare to her thoughtless new boss.

A large jeep was tearing across the sand, bearing down upon them at a rapid speed.

'Well done!' Chris Stephens smiled broadly at the two white-coated men who jumped out on to the sand carrying a stretcher. 'You'd better go with the patient, Sister. I've got to drive my own car back. I'll meet you at the clinic.'

'My clothes?' Only now did it register that she was inadequately clad for a nursing sister. Fine on the beach, but if she was on her way back to civilisation she needed to gather up the pile of hastily discarded clothing.

The doctor grinned as he sprinted across the beach, retrieved the sandy pile and tossed them across to her. 'Put them on in the jeep.'

Hastily she pulled the cotton dress over her bikini, promising herself a long, soothing shower to rinse off the salty sea as soon as she had settled her patient.

The jeep bumped along a narrow road that led directly from the beach. The clinic was barely three hundred yards from the sea.

Only a couple of hours before, when she had first arrived there, Sara had deposited her luggage at the reception area and made straight for the sea to cool off. The Indonesian nurse/receptionist had been unable to give her any information about her boss's whereabouts and seemed to have absolutely no idea what to do with her. No one, it seemed, had been advised of her arrival.

The same nurse came forward now as the jeep stopped in the unloading area.

'Dr Stephens was asking for you, Sister Freeman,' she began.

'He found me,' Sara told her tersely. Time enough for recriminations later. 'Help me get this patient into a cool room. Do you have air-conditioning here?'

'But of course.' Chris Stephens, who had come up behind her, was smiling. 'We have all the latest technology here in my clinic. I'll show you round later. Meanwhile, let's get our patient into Intensive Care.'

As she settled her patient in, Sara was truly amazed at the small Intensive Care Unit. Apart from the bamboo screens beside the louvred windows and the intensely cold, air-conditioned temperature, she could have imagined she was in the ICU department of her own teaching hospital in London. She felt a sense of relief. After the fiasco of her arrival she hadn't known what to expect.

Before she left her patient in the capable hands of the Indonesian nurses, she was rewarded by the flickering of his eyes and then a partial return to consciousness.

'He'll be OK,' Chris Stephens assured her. 'Go and get yourself sorted out, Sister. Ask the reception nurse to take you to your quarters. If you surface in time for a sundowner I'll be in the bar. OK?'

She was taken aback by his casual manner. No apology had been offered for not meeting her. No polite questioning about her long journey from England. And now the assumption that she would like to join him for a sundowner!

She looked up into the cool brown eyes and, in spite of herself, she liked what she saw. A handsome face, and he knew it. The man was full of confidence, almost bordering on arrogance. Here was a man who was used to getting his own way with women.

But not this woman, she thought. Since Mike's death she hadn't looked at another man, and she wasn't about to start now. But she might go and have a drink with him, if only to find out why her arrival had been overlooked.

'I need some rest, but if I feel up to it I'll meet you this evening,' she heard herself saying, amazed at how friendly the words sounded.

The winning smile expanded to reveal strong, dazzlingly white teeth. 'Suit yourself,' Chris Stephens said in an easygoing voice before turning away and giving his full attention to the patient.

I really do need some rest, Sara thought as she followed the nurse/receptionist along the winding paths that led through the clinic gardens to her quarters. Her luggage, she was told, had already been installed. Another example of the unexpected efficiency of the clinic helped to raise it in her estimation.

As she looked around her at the gardens, she felt her spirits lifting.

'It's so beautiful here!' she exclaimed.

The Indonesian nurse smiled at Sara's enthusiasm.

'Dr Stephens likes his patients to be surrounded by beauty. We have many gardeners to care for the gardens.'

They were crossing an ornamental wooden bridge

over a clear running stream. Sara paused and held on to the balustrade in the middle of the bridge as she stared down, amazed at the size of the golden fish swimming below her. A huge frog, basking on a large green leaf in the middle of the stream, seemed to wink at her in the sunlight, as if welcoming her to his tropical paradise. And all around her the scent of the exotic flowers and shrubs assailed her senses.

'It's hard to believe this is a clinic,' she said to the nurse. 'I presume the patients are housed in those thatched-roof cottages?'

'That is correct,' the young woman agreed. 'They are similar to our staff cottages. And you have been allocated one of the nicest ones.' She gave a shy smile. 'We are a hospitable people and we like to make sure that guests on Bali are happy.'

They had moved along through the fragrant gardens, the path twisting and turning until they reached a high stone wall that marked the boundary of the clinic. Walking along beside the wall, they came to a secluded corner where there were only two cottages.

'This is Dr Stephens' cottage, and the one at the end is for you, Sister Freeman.'

'It's lovely!'

Sara's hazel eyes shone with admiration as she viewed the small thatched cottage from the outside. She stepped on to the tiles of the square terrace that led to the ornately carved wooden door.

The nurse opened the door, handed her the key and then went away, with a brief reminder that Sister only had to pick up her phone to call for anything she required to be brought to her cottage.

Sara closed the door, leaning against it as she revelled in the cool, air-conditioned atmosphere. Her eyelids were drooping. She would lie down on the inviting bed and investigate the place later. Half an hour would be all she needed. . .

The bedside phone was shrilling. Where on earth was she? What time was it?

'So, you decided to stand me up, did you?'

Sara recognised Chris Stephens' voice and her mind began ticking over again.

'No more than you deserve,' she snapped back before she could stop herself. 'You didn't exactly make a great effort to welcome me when I first arrived.'

She heard a low, throaty chuckle.

'Something came up; I couldn't get there in time. Can I buy you dinner to make up for it?'

'I'm not sure.'

'Tell you what: while you're deciding we'll go and have a look at the sunset on the beach. You've got ten minutes to throw on some clothes and then I'll pick you up. I'm only next door. But hurry, because the sun won't wait, and neither will I.'

CHAPTER TWO

THE sun was suspended in the sky by shimmering chains of light. But, even as she watched, Sara saw the great fiery globe slipping down towards the waves. The sea was bathed in a golden glow as it waited for the swift descent. Lower and lower the sun fell until it dived beneath the waves, leaving only a faint iridescent shimmer on the surface.

It was a few seconds before she could find her voice and then it croaked hoarsely, affected by the emotion she had experienced during the spectacular sunset. It was a long time since she had been deeply moved.

'I'm so glad you brought me here.'

Her words sounded banal even to her own ears. She wondered what her boss would make of them. She turned to look up at him in the twilight, noting the arrogant thrust of his chin, the high angular cheekbones that contoured his good-looking face. His light brown, sun-streaked hair, sleeked back when he had arrived at her cottage to bring her down here on to the beach, was now creeping over his wide forehead towards the gold-framed designer sunglasses.

She remembered, with a feeling of embarrassment, how he had insisted they both wear sunglasses to watch the sunset, and she had delayed their departure even further by an undignified scramble into her battered old suitcase while Chris Stephens viewed the spectacle from her doorway, an amused smile hovering on his lips. He was so sure of himself that he made her nervous.

'I knew you'd enjoy it. Bali is renowned for its sunsets, and out here on the beach they're particularly good.' He paused. 'So, have you forgiven me for leaving you stranded at the airport? I'd like to take you out to dinner, but not if you're still mad at me.'

Sara smiled up at him and felt the strangest sensation in the pit of her stomach. It was a long time since she had had to consider a dinner invitation. Oh, there had been the occasional trip to the theatre with one of the doctors at St Celine's followed by supper if it wasn't too late. And one of the consultants had taken her to concerts at the Festival Hall several times, until she had discovered that he was divorced and desperately seeking someone to help him out with his teenage children. She had known that it was only a matter of time before he proposed marriage, and that was the last thing she wanted. But, standing here on the beach with this comparative stranger, she felt the beginnings of an excited tingling in her veins.

'Dinner would be a good idea,' she said. 'I'm starving!'

Chris smiled. 'As good a reason as any. I'll take you to Made's Restaurant.'

The restaurant opened on to the busy street that was thronged with nocturnal revellers. There were two storeys, both packed with a cosmopolitan clientele. At first glance, Sara had the definite impression that this was the place to be seen in Kuta. All the beautiful people came here: artists, musicians, fashion designers, and actors resting from their run in the West End who were wondering what to do with themselves if that long-awaited phone call didn't come.

Chris Stephens put his hand under her elbow and led her towards wide wooden steps that led steeply up into the higher elevation. From their corner table they were able to look down over the balustrade at the whirl of social activity, watching the people come and go, listening to the laughter and the chatter that somehow made itself heard above the background music.

The waitress who came to their table was a pretty blonde, and she gave Chris Stephens a dazzling smile.

'Hi, Doc, what can I get you this evening?'

Sara noticed the hint of an American accent overloaded with another more foreign one. Probably Swedish, she deduced, as she accepted the menu.

'First we'll have some champagne, Brigitte. The one I had last time I was here. . .and make it ice-cold.'

The girl smiled. 'But of course, Doctor.'

'I'll have a dozen oysters to start with. How about you, Sister?'

'I'd like some asparagus,' said Sara. 'And a steak to follow.'

The doctor nodded approvingly. 'Good choice. The steaks here are excellent. How do you like yours?'

The menu was quickly sorted out; the champagne arrived; Chris Stephens raised his glass towards Sara.

'Have you forgiven me enough to drop the Doctor bit and call me Chris?' he asked.

She smiled, her earlier distress forgotten as she found

herself swayed by his charming manner. 'Of course. . . and you must call me Sara.'

'I intend to.' He smiled at her over the rim of his glass.

'Incidentally, what was the problem about meeting me?' she asked ingenuously.

The hint of a frown crossed his handsome face. 'I thought we'd established that fact. I had another more pressing commitment.'

'And you couldn't get someone else to meet me?' She tried to make her words sound light; her own inbred good manners made it impossible to understand his cavalier attitude.

Chris put down his glass. 'By the time I realised I couldn't make it I was in a situation where it was impossible to call the clinic. OK? Do you think that could be the end of the inquisition?'

'I'm sorry,' said Sara quietly.

She hated herself for apologising as soon as she'd said it, but he was, after all, her boss, and she knew she had better watch her step. She desperately needed this job, and there had been dozens of applicants for it. If there was a clash of personalities and Chris Stephens asked her to leave he would have no problem in replacing her.

'That's OK. You were understandably tired and worried,' he said, easily.

She swallowed her retort.

'So tell me about yourself.' He leaned back against his chair, his deep brown eyes narrowing as he watched her.

She was sitting beneath one of the overhead fans, for

which she was grateful, because it was a hot, humid evening and she could feel the fabric of her shirt sticking to her skin. Far better to have worn cotton, she thought, making a mental note for future occasions.

'I thought you would have read my CV,' she began carefully.

His eyes glinted dangerously as he replied.

'That only told me that you were well qualified for this post...may I say over-qualified, if the truth be known. Which is why I want to know what made you come out here. I know you're a widow. What I'm wondering is if you've come out to forget or to look for another husband.'

Sara took a sip of her champagne to calm herself. 'You certainly don't mince your words, Doctor... Chris. I don't see that it has anything to do with you why I'm here. Let's say I needed a change.'

'To get away from a boyfriend?' he persisted.

'Absolutely not! Oh, well, if you must know, there was someone, considerably older than me, who had designs on my future. But apart from going to concerts we had nothing in common, and I certainly didn't want to spend the rest of my life looking after someone else's children, even if it would have solved all my financial problems.'

Chris refilled her glass before leaning back in his chair, his eyes studying her.

She found herself smiling as she felt the tension between them relaxing. 'I'm loosening up, aren't I? It must be the champagne.'

He leaned across the table and took hold of the ends

of her fingers with his own. Gently he stroked them towards the nails before leaning back again in his chair.

She experienced the strangest feeling. Her hands were tingling as she listened to his deep, sonorous voice, raised now above the music so that she could clearly hear him.

'You're too tense, Sara,' he told her. 'I'm not trying to pry, but as your employer I need to know more about you. For example, I don't know how long you've been widowed. If it was recently then I'll have to handle you like Dresden china.'

She took a deep breath. 'Your concern is touching,' she told him, sensing that her sarcasm was lost on him. 'I've been widowed three years and I'm very tough. There's no need to give me any more concern than you would to the rest of your staff.'

'Well, that's a relief.' He smiled, a relaxed boyish smile that helped to melt away some of her renewed antagonism. 'That's all I need to know for the moment. Let's just enjoy ourselves. The night is young.'

He clinked his glass with hers.

'My husband, Mike, used to say that,' she said in a faraway voice, not sure whether her companion could hear her or not. 'The night is young,' she repeated softly, feeling as if she were taking part in a dream. . . an unpleasant dream, bordering on a nightmare.

Chris leaned across the table. 'Are you all right, Sara?'

She nodded. 'Yes, I think so. I was just remembering something from the past.'

'Nostalgia can be terribly disturbing. Your husband sounds as if he was a lot of fun. I expect that's what's been missing in your life since he died. Purely from a medical point of view, I'm going to prescribe a large dose of fun. . .for this evening, at any rate.'

From then on, Sara found herself swept along by his infectious bonhomie. He told her jokes that made her laugh so much that it was difficult to find time to eat the delicious food. He regaled her with stories of his life as a medical student at St Teresa's in London, until she'd built up a picture of a harum-scarum individual who was lucky to have passed his finals. It was only when he let slip the fact that he had come first in his year for surgery and consequently been offered a surgical post he didn't want that she began to think there was more to Chris Stephens than met the eye.

'But why didn't you stay in London and continue a career in surgery?' she asked, pushing aside her plate, which still had half a succulent steak on it.

His eyes clouded over, but his tone remained bantering. 'Why indeed? Why does anyone do anything in this world? What are you doing out here? No, don't answer that. I'll get the bill and we'll move on. I want to show you the Kuta night-life. It will be good for you . . .it'll take you out of yourself, because heaven knows, that's what you need.'

He took her to a disco, leading her by the hand through winding streets illuminated by neon signs and garish flashing lights.

'I haven't been in a disco for years,' she told him as they were ushered to a table near to a small square that served as a dance floor.

He laughed. 'Exactly! That's what's missing in your

life—fun, freedom, enjoyment. You've come to the right place.'

Two glasses of pale-coloured fluid were placed on their table.

'On the house, Doc,' said the waiter, a young man sporting several gold earrings in one ear.

'Thanks, Tom,' Chris replied, raising his glass and taking a tentative sip.

Before Sara could decide what to do with hers, she was whisked off towards the dance floor.

'I told you, I haven't danced since I was a teenager,' she said to Chris as he twirled her around.

'Oh, you poor old thing! Five whole years without dancing should be a criminal offence!'

The beat of the music was becoming more insistent. She let herself go with the rhythm and felt the exhilaration coursing throug her body. When Chris eventually led her back to their table she was breathless with the dancing and the laughter.

She took a sip of her drink and pulled a face.

'Don't drink it—it's called an Arak Attack,' Chris told her, a wide boyish grin on his face. 'I just wanted to see your first reaction to it. It's one of the local drinks, but it can be lethal stuff if you're not used to it. Tom was only trying to be hospitable when he brought it for us.'

'Do you come here often?' she asked.

They both laughed at the clichéd question.

'I have to,' he replied.

'How do you mean, you have to?'

He smiled. 'I wish you wouldn't ask so many questions! Let me order some champagne.'

He was already glancing around, trying to attract the attention of one of the waiters.

'No more, really,' she protested. 'I'd like to go back.'

He hesitated. 'Your wish is my command, o, Princess.'

They walked back through the streets. The air of gaiety and happiness was getting through to her. It seemed perfectly natural that Chris should hold her by the hand to steer her through the revelling crowds. And she liked the touch of his fingers more than she cared to admit. But she wished he would drop the bantering tone and be serious for a few minutes. She had absolutely no idea what he was like beneath this outward veneer.

They walked back through the gardens which seemed like a haven of quiet compared with the razzmatazz of the surrounding streets.

'It reminds me of my convent school,' she said. 'High stone walls keeping out the riff-raff. Once we step through the gate we're in a different world.'

'You're right. And that's how I like it. It's good for my patients. Talking of which, I'd like to check up on our young man who nearly drowned. Would you like to come with me?'

She looked up at his face, outlined in the moonlight, and saw that he was serious at last.

'I most certainly would,' she told him.

The Intensive Care Unit was quiet. Only the occasional whirring of the equipment disturbed the peace and calm.

The Indonesian nurse gave them a full report before they went in to see the patient.

Sara had been right about the patient's age. He was twenty-one. His name was Nick Cramer and he was travelling around the Far East on some sort of extended holiday. He was now fully conscious and asking to be let out, but the nurse had insisted he remained until Chris had seen him.

Nick Cramer was sitting on the edge of his bed, shivering. A young male nurse was trying to persuade him to drink a glass of water, without success.

'You can leave us for a few minutes, Nurse,' said Chris in a casual tone.

As soon as the door was closed he sat down beside the patient. Gently he took hold of his head and raised it so that he could get a good look.

Sara stifled the gasp that threatened to spring to her lips when she noticed the telltale symptoms. Above the unkempt beard, Nick Cramer had watery eyes and a running nose. He was holding his stomach in an effort to soothe away the obvious stomach cramps.

'What are you on, Nick?' Chris asked gently.

The young man's teeth were chattering as he attempted to reply. 'Anything I can get — and I need a fix quickly. Heroin, cocaine, morphine, pethidine. . . come on, Doc, this is a hospital. . .you must have something you can give me!'

'I'll get you some Methadone,' Chris told him quietly, standing up and going towards the door. 'Sister will take care of you till I get back.'

'Methadone!' the patient sniffed, in a disparaging

tone. 'That's what they gave me at the treatment centre. It won't do anything for me.'

'Well, it will be a step in the right direction,' said Chris, walking quickly away down the corridor.

Sara was glad he'd left the door open. She put out her hand and took hold of her patient's, trying to calm him. The shivering continued.

'I vowed I'd never go through this again. They couldn't cure me in England, so I came out here on a one-way trip. But it only made things worse. I can't live without a fix. When I swam out in the sea I didn't intend to come back. I must have blacked out. And then some idiot went and brought me back to the shore!'

He was crying now. Sara put her arm around the broad shoulders. 'Hush, we'll soon have you well again,' she said, trying to convince herself as well as the desperate patient.

Chris returned and gave their patient a large dose of Methadone.

They stayed on until the effects of the drug were evident.

'Tomorrow we'll talk about your long-term prospects,' Chris said, as they prepared to leave.

'What long-term prospects?' the young man asked, in an apathetic voice.

Sara patted Nick's hand. 'I'll come in to see you in the morning,' she told him.

He turned his face away from her.

Chris left instructions with the male nurse that their patient must not be left alone. And he urged that he be treated with extreme kindness and courtesy.

'If it's something you can't handle in the night, give me a call,' he said.

They walked back across the gardens. Sara was saddened by the revelation that her patient had tried to take his own life.

'I hope he won't try again,' she said to Chris as he accompanied her to her door.

His eyes were serious as he looked down at her in the moonlight.

'Drug addicts are very unpredictable. I've had a lot of experience with them, and I know that you can't tell from one minute to the next what they're going to do.'

He held out his hand. 'Give me your key.' He unlocked the door and stood back. 'Sleep well, Sister Sara. Sweet dreams.'

And then he was gone.

She heard his footsteps receding as he walked back along the gravel path that led to his nearby cottage.

'Sweet dreams,' he'd said. Sara smiled. Had he any idea how he had stirred up her dreams? Dreams and nightmares from the past that she'd hoped were long forgotten.

CHAPTER THREE

IN HER dream she was waiting for Mike to come home. He had promised to be early, but she had her doubts. There was a pounding on the door. She didn't want to open it; if the door remained closed she wouldn't know the truth. The noise of the hammering blows on the door was getting louder...and something else. Overhead she could hear the whirring of the helicopters flying low over the house. This time there was no escape...

She tried to scream, and the effort wakened her. She was making a strangled cry as she sat up in her unfamiliar bed. It was the noise of the air-conditioning that had set off the familiar nightmare. She got off the bed and ran over to switch it off. Far better to sweat it out through the night than risk being transported to the past again. She glanced at the fan in the ceiling. That would be even worse.

She went through into the bathroom and stood under the cold shower. As the soothing water cascaded over her she became calmer. It was only a dream, after all. Dreams couldn't hurt you. They never had done in the past three years.

She stepped out of the shower and pulled a large fluffy towel around her. They certainly went in for luxury at this place!

She noticed that the bathroom was like an indoor

garden. It was circular, and part of it was open to the stars, although covered over with the thin mesh designed to keep out the mosquitoes. There was actual soil in the flower beds, and a tiny gravel path leading from the bathing area to a small drying area where she could hang her underwear and swimming things. It was definitely a step up from the tiny room she'd had in the sisters' quarters at St Celine's.

As she thought about her little room back in London she felt a pang of nostalgia for the place. It had been a good thing she'd kept it on after her marriage. There were all those occasions when she had been unable to trek back to the wilds of Essex to the huge house that Mike had insisted on buying; that millstone round their necks which had finally broken them. But throughout all the troubled times she had continued to commute to London, and then, when she was finally alone and the house was gone, she'd lived all the time in her little room. It had been her haven of retreat, a place where she could close the door on the prying world.

She smiled as her sense of proportion returned. She went back into the bedroom and climbed on to the bed. Rather like this place will become, she thought. Only this is much grander. . .and the man next door is far too disturbing.

As she lay stretched out on the bed, trying to remain cool, she remembered the touch of Chris's fingers at the table in the restaurant—smooth, confident, capable surgeon's fingers. They had affected her more than she cared to admit. Senses that had lain dormant for so long had been aroused.

She gave herself a mental shake. It wasn't safe to

encourage this feeling of relaxation. She had to remain on her guard.

For the next month Sara studiously avoided all social contact with Chris. He issued casual invitations for supper in the evenings, walks on the beach, a drink in the bar beside the clinic swimming pool; but she declined them all, telling herself that he asked too many questions; he disturbed her emotionally. She couldn't risk becoming too close to him, or, what would be far worse, becoming dependent on him. She had to keep her independence and secrecy at all costs.

Their drug patient, Nick Cramer, was a constant problem to them. Whatever they did for him it was never enough. He complained constantly and begged to be allowed to have some morphine. But Chris was firm with him, reducing the dosage of Methadone gradually, always hoping to rehabilitate the young man.

'You're very patient with Nick,' Sara said one day when their patient had been particularly trying. 'How long do you intend keeping him here?'

Chris smiled. 'As long as it takes. I've told him he's free to go, but he's decided he wants to stay on.'

'He knows when he's found a soft billet,' she said. 'It's much easier staying on here being looked after than going out to face the world on your own. Who's going to pay his bill?'

Chris shrugged. 'I'm not counting. He's an interesting case, and I can afford to take on a few freebies.'

'It's a constant source of amazement to me how you make this place pay,' she told him.

The flicker of a frown crossed Chris's finely chiselled

features. 'I don't think it's any concern of yours how I make the place pay. You're paid to work here, not to act as an accountant.'

'I'm sorry.'

Again, the apology hurt her, but she realised she had overstepped the mark once more. His words disturbed her. She had heard the same argument so many times before in her life. Don't worry about money; it's no concern of yours. Chris was a voice from the past, and she didn't like it.

She was puzzled by the whole set-up here at the Lotus Clinic. There were whole days when Chris didn't put in an appearance, when he simply disappeared; vague messages were left with the reception nurse to the effect that he'd been called away up country.

As if reading her thoughts, Chris began to explain. 'Not only do I make the place pay, but I also help the local medical service. No doubt you've been wondering about my trips up country. Maybe you'd like to see some of the work we do out in the field? Be ready early tomorrow and you can replace my usual clinic nurse when we go out on a vaccination round.'

They set off at six the next day in a large black Land Rover, Sara in her white sister's uniform with the small cap on the back of her head and Chris in white trousers and short-sleeved cotton shirt open at the neck.

'Got to look the part,' he explained with a grin as he put his foot down on the accelerator.

Clouds of dust flew up behind them as they left the narrow streets of Kuta far behind and headed north. Rice terraces carved out of the hills spilled down towards the paddy fields of the plain. And ever in the distance the tall mountains brooded beneath the billowing clouds.

'The scenery is magnificent. . .breathtaking,' Sara remarked, after they had been travelling for over an hour.

Chris took his eyes from the road for a few seconds and gave her a warm smile. 'The magic of Bali is getting through to you at last! I knew it would.'

Their destination was a small clinic, held in the village of Bakatu, not far from the temple of Tanah Lot. All through the day a never-ending stream of patients arrived. The majority were children for routine vaccination. This was what the clinic was supposed to be on that day, but neither of them felt inclined to turn away the other medical problems that were presented to them.

Often it was the mother who brought the children, sometimes it was the grandmother or an aunt. But in many cases they brought small gifts for Chris and Sara . . .a couple of eggs, some flowers. On one occasion a child presented them with a small monkey which they had to decline, although with many thanks for the kind thought.

In the middle of the afternoon, an old lady hurried into the clinic and persuaded Chris and Sara to follow her. There were only two patients waiting for them at the time, so they asked them to stay on until they got back. The old woman was muttering something about her daughter, who was apparently in terrible pain. It was obvious that all was not well.

It wasn't until they reached the small village house

only yards from the clinic that they realised that the daughter was in labour. Sara followed Chris into a small back room where a woman lay stretched out on the wooden bed.

There was no time to scrub up, no time for any of the usual preparations. The baby's head was presenting itself. Sara turned to request that the mother-to be start panting, but she had no need to offer advice. Her patient knew exactly what to do.

Three children in varying sizes were peeping around the door waiting for the arrival of their new baby brother or sister. The grandmother shooed them away as she went in search of more hot water.

'It's a boy!' Sara announced, only minutes after their arrival, and Chris translated the good news to the mother, who beamed with happiness.

The cord was cut, the baby wrapped in a sheet and presented to the mother.

When all the usual cleansing and checking procedures had been accomplished they were invited to have tea with the family. It was strong black tea, served in a brightly painted mug, and Sara found it most welcome. The mother, she noticed, was already sitting up and taking control of her family again. The grandmother had been relegated to her position of second-in-command as the children admired their new brother. There was no sign of the father. Probably he would be told of the addition to his family when he returned from the rice fields in the evening.

In barely an hour they were back at the clinic.

'I can't see why we were called out at all,' Sara said. 'The mother and the grandmother had everything under control. I expect they produced the other children without any outside help.'

Chris smiled. 'I expect you're right. But they do like to make use of us if we're in the area. I get called upon for all kinds of medical problems when I'm out in the field, especially up there in the mountains.'

She heard the catch in his voice, saw the way his eyes strayed to the window that looked out towards the mysterious hills shrouded in mist. One day she hoped he would take her up there. Because she had the strangest feeling that this particular field trip wasn't typical of his work. He was hiding something from her, and she meant to find out what it was.

It was almost sundown when the stream of patients ceased and Sara was able to pack up the boxes and cases and go outside to help Chris with the loading.

'How often do you do this?' she asked, breathing in the cooling air.

'It depends on the medical authorities at the Rumah Sakit—that's the hospital. I work closely with them. They phone me up and ask me if I'm free, and we take it from there. Thanks for your help today,' he added. 'I thought you'd enjoy some field work after being cooped up at the clinic for your first couple of weeks.'

'Oh, I get out occasionally,' she told him, handing up a particularly heavy case of syringes and medicines. 'Be careful with this one—it's fragile.'

'Half an hour to sunset,' Chris observed quietly.

She paused, watching him loading the case at the back of the jeep.

'It will be dark then before we get back,' she remarked in a matter-of-fact tone.

'That doesn't matter. I was wondering whether we could get down to the temple in time to watch the sunset.'

She smiled. 'You love the Balinese sunsets, don't you?'

'Don't you?' He had finished loading and was watching her.

'I suppose I'm a romantic at heart,' she replied, suddenly feeling a surge of colour rushing to her cheeks.

'But you keep it well hidden. You give the impression that you'd rather die than give in to your emotions.'

'Do I? How strange!' She knew it wasn't strange at all. Chris was one of the most perceptive individuals she'd met in a long time. A close relationship with a man like this would be dangerous. . .impossible.

'Jump in,' he ordered. 'We might make it.'

The road to the sea was winding, bumpy, unpredictable.

'It's not doing much for the springs!' Sara called above the noise of the engine.

He laughed. 'We've got good shock-absorbers on this one. I need them when I travel around up country.'

And then, as they rounded a bend in the road, the full beauty of the seascape lay spread out in front of them. Wave after wave was pounding on to the shore in the twilight. And beyond, completely surrounded by the sea, the mysterious temple of Tanah Lot nestled on a huge brown rock, forming a striking silhouette against the crimson and gold of the evening sky. The last rays of the sun lingered fleetingly on the leaves of the trees surrounding the ancient temple as if offering the final blessing of the day.

'Quick! The sun will be gone in seconds.'

Chris caught her hand and swept her down the slope towards the beach. And then they were running over the soft sand towards the sea. The sun was sinking on the south side of the temple rock, making its last appearance, tantalisingly low in the sky. It seemed to hold steady for a few seconds to give them time to catch their breath, and then it was gone, plunging the shore into semi-darkness.

Chris turned towards her and took both her hands in his. 'Spectacular, wasn't it?'

She nodded, her heart too full for words.

'I shouldn't torment you like this,' he said, after a few seconds had elapsed and neither of them had spoken. 'I suppose it's only natural that you should think of your husband at times like this.'

Sara raised her eyes to his. 'Yes, it's only natural,' she repeated, in a faraway voice. 'But it's something I have to come to terms with.'

'Time is a great healer,' he told her gently.

'That's what everyone tells me,' she said. How could she tell him that these platitudes only made things worse? 'Let's go back now.'

Chris steered the jeep back over the bumpy roads, his eyes glued to the glare of his headlights that lit up the way along the dark narrow roads.

'Would you like to have a late supper?' he asked when they arrived back at the hospital. 'Nothing very grand, just a sandwich at one of the bars that likes to call itself a pub. It's a cross between something from the Australian outback and ye olde village pub in the Home Counties.'

Sara smiled. She didn't want to be on her own tonight, that was for sure. Something about spending a whole day with Chris. It was disturbing. . .it was dangerous. . .but suddenly she felt like living dangerously! After all, where had all this caution got her in the last three years?

'Sounds good to me,' she smiled. 'Give me half an hour to shower and change.'

He was sitting on her terrace drinking a cold beer when she went out. 'I decided to make myself at home, not knowing how long it would take you to transform yourself,' he explained.

She enjoyed the look of admiration in his eyes as he surveyed her. She'd taken longer than usual to dress, but the time had been worth it. She wanted to look good for him.

Her stone-coloured safari pants had been pressed by the maid, along with the cream linen shirt. Her strappy sandals lifted her up to chin level when Chris stood up. At five feet five she felt she needed a little more height so that she could reach up to the rarefied atmosphere of her companion. And she had tied her mid-brown hair back in a ponytail. It made her look younger than her twenty-five years, but it also made her feel more carefree than the usual chignon she wore on duty.

She felt Chris's hand under her elbow, and a little frisson of excitement ran through her as they made their way along the garden paths between the tropical plants and flowers. The scent of the petals and leaves mingled in the night air, forming a natural perfume that went straight to her head. It was more intoxicating than the champagne they had drunk on her first evening in Bali.

I'm letting down my guard, she thought nervously. But somehow, tonight it didn't seem to matter.

They ordered chicken sandwiches and beer. The sandwiches turned out to be huge and impossible to put into the mouth. Sara finished up eating hers with a knife and fork. The music was loud, impossibly loud.

'Let's go for a walk on the beach!' shouted Chris.

'Good idea!'

The beach was deserted. Tourists and locals alike were in the town. They walked slowly side by side; he didn't try to hold her hand.

'So, do you think you'll be able to forget?' he asked, after a few minutes of companionable silence.

'I shall never be able to forget,' she told him softly.

He stopped, taking hold of her hands and staring down at her.

She had taken off her high-heeled shoes and was walking barefoot across the still warm sand. She felt small again as she looked up into his eyes, those strong expressive eyes that seemed to pierce inside her in the moonlight.

'He must have been a great character. Never is a long time to carry the torch for one man, however wonderful he was. You really should try to forget. Until you forget, you can't begin to have a life of your own. . .to start a new relationship.'

She saw the tender expression in his eyes. Oh, if only she could! If only she could take this man at face value. . .fall for him as she'd fallen for Mike in those first heady months.

She swallowed hard, the tears springing to her eyes. She ran a hand over her face to compose herself.

Chris bent down and touched her cheek lightly with his lips. 'Don't cry, Sara. You'll get over him in time. It was a good idea to come away like this. I'll help you all I can, because I can't bear to see you unhappy like this.'

She lifted her hand and put it over his lips. 'Hush! You don't understand.'

How could she tell him that when Mike died she had felt nothing but relief? Her love had died a long time before, killed by the lies and the deceit. But she had never admitted this to anyone. She had guarded the memories of when their love had been new; when Mike had swept her off her feet. 'Let's have fun,' was his constant cry. 'Money no object. . .let's go!'

She came back to the present as she watched the tender expression in Chris's eyes and wondered if she could trust him. The parallels of the situation were too strikingly similar.

But even as she wondered, he lowered his head and kissed her firmly on the lips. For an instant she resisted, and then the sensuous, instinctive arousal deep within her took over. She moulded her body against his chest as he pulled her into his arms. It was as if she had known him all her life. . .

CHAPTER FOUR

SARA was relieved that Chris had gone up into the hills again. It gave her time to review her feelings about him. The morning after their walk on Kuta Beach she had been appalled at how easily she had given in to her pent-up emotions. When Chris had gathered her into his arms, she'd closed her eyes and shut out all thoughts of the past. For several moments she'd felt like a young girl again. . .like the girl she used to be before Mike came into her life.

Now, two weeks later, she'd had time to think, and she was determined to be more careful where Chris was concerned. It was his devil-may-care attitude to life that reminded her so much of Mike and all the problems his recklessness had brought her. But physically, she reflected, Chris was quite different from Mike. Mike's hair had been blond and flyaway, his skin inclined to freckles in the summer. And Mike had been shorter than Chris but much stockier. Chris was the lean, athletic type, suntanned, his brown eyes dark and mysterious.

As Sara thought about Chris's dark, secretive eyes she gave an involuntary shiver. She shouldn't have looked up into them on that night, before he took her into his arms. He'd only been giving her the sympathy any human being would offer to a young widow until that point when their eyes had met.

'Are you OK, Sister?'

She looked up from the case notes she had been studying in her tiny office overlooking the clinic garden. Staff Nurse Preston, one of the Australian nurses, was standing in the doorway, her amiable face creased with concern. Sara always left her door open so that staff and patients could come and go as they pleased. This part of the clinic didn't have air-conditioning, but there were huge fans in the ceiling and the bamboo doors were rarely closed, allowing the occasional sea breeze to waft inside.

'I'm fine,' Sara said quickly, assuming a professional smile. 'Did you want to see me, Molly?'

The staff nurse hesitated. 'Well, I did, but you were looking so worried just now, I thought maybe I'd come back later.'

'Come on in,' invited Sara, motioning to one of the wicker chairs near the long windows that led out on to the veranda. 'I can finish these later.'

She gathered up the case notes and pushed them to one side. If the truth be known, she had been staring at the same piece of paper for several minutes while her mind revolved around the problem of her new boss. She resolved to take the notes back to her room that evening and study them in her own time when perhaps she would have more powers of concentration.

'It's about Nick Cramer,' Molly Preston began. 'I'm worried about him. He's asking for something stronger than Methadone, and Dr Stephens gave me explicit instructions that he was to be given low-dosage Methadone and weaned off that as soon as possible. It's easier said than done. I mean, Dr Stephens has gone swanning off into the hills again—heaven knows what he finds to do up there—leaving the rest of us with difficult patients to cope with, and. . .'

'Have you spoken to Dr Cassandra?' Sara put in quickly. 'Dr Stephens left her in charge.'

Molly Preston gave a disparaging shrug of her ample shoulders. 'She's worse than useless. Always sticks by the book and insists on obeying Dr Stephens' every whim. If you ask me, she's besotted by the man.'

'I must admit the thought had crossed my mind as well,' Sara said sympathetically.

Dr Cassandra Smithson, in her early thirties, was of Anglo-Indian parentage, small, demure, dark-skinned, with big brown eyes that remained calm in every crisis. She was sure of herself and totally loyal to Chris Stephens. Sara had only once tried to question the woman doctor's authority, and had received a chilling rebuke. She had come to the conclusion that Dr Cassandra would listen only to her boss on matters of medical policy. In her eyes he could do no wrong.

Sara gave a reluctant smile. 'There's nothing I can do if Dr Cassandra won't help you. I know I'm technically in charge of the nursing staff, but my hands are tied on matters of medical policy. When Dr Stephens gets back. . .'

'And when will that be?' Molly Preston burst in impatiently.

Sara gave a resigned shrug of her shoulders. 'Your guess is as good as mine. You've worked here longer than I have. How long do these expeditions usually last?'

The staff nurse ran a hand through her short auburn

hair, repinning the white cap that threatened to fall off. 'Anything from two days to a month. Sometimes I wish I'd stayed home in Australia. At least the work was predictable in my old hospital.'

'So what made you leave?' asked Sara, anxious to form a basis of companionship with this competent nurse. On several occasions she had found her extremely helpful and knew she was going to need all the help she could get if she was to make a go of her new job.

'I wanted to travel and get paid for it,' Molly Preston replied with a wry grin. 'How about you?'

For a moment Sara was taken aback, but then the plump, round, friendly face looking at her encouraged her to open up.

'I lost my husband three years ago; I was getting in a rut and needed a change. Like you, I thought it would be nice to travel and get paid for it. It's the only way I'll get to see the world.'

'So your husband didn't leave you a fortune so that you could be a lady of leisure?' Molly Preston's face was dimpled with fun.

Sara leaned back in her chair, a wry grin on her face. 'Quite the opposite. He left me a legacy of debts. . . but I'll get them paid off if I keep on working,' she added hurriedly, wondering why she was being so open. Maybe it was the Australian's disarming manner. She had a directness that was refreshingly honest.

'You're young to be a widow. How did your husband die?'

Sara took a deep breath as the memories came flooding back. 'Mike was killed in a car crash.'

'How awful! Were you with him at the time?'

Sara swallowed hard, clenching her hands beneath the desk.

'No, I was at home. Mike was returning. . .returning from a business trip. . .and the car went out of control.' She could feel her voice beginning to shake. 'Look, I'd rather not talk about it, if you don't mind.'

'Of course. I didn't mean to pry. How long were you married?'

'Two years.' Sara's voice was under control again.

Molly pulled a sympathetic face. 'Ah, that's awful! Barely got the honeymoon over with. You must miss him terribly.'

Sara drew in her breath. 'Life will never be the same, that's for sure. . .and now, about our patient. Perhaps if I come along with you now. . .'

'I hoped you'd say that, Sister,' the staff nurse said.

They walked together out into the reception area. All the administrative offices were grouped around here. From the reception area there was a corridor that led to the main medical units which housed the patients requiring specialist treatment. For the more convalescent type of patient there were the small thatched cottages set in the clinic gardens.

Nick Cramer, of course, was still in the medical unit, under constant supervision. Sara found him sitting by the window of his room, staring out at the flower-bedecked veranda, a vacant expression on his bearded face.

'How are you feeling today, Nick?' Sara asked briskly. She had found that a namby-pamby approach didn't work with this patient. You had to be firm but kind.

'How do you think?' the young man answered sullenly. 'Had my Methadone cut by half, and I feel lousy. Might as well go out and drown myself.'

A sudden image of Nick's contorted face on the sand when she had first seen him shot into Sara's mind. She couldn't let that happen again. She was convinced there was more they could do for this unfortunate young man.

'Well, if you're going to give in so easily, I suppose there's no point wasting our time with you,' she said, hoping to call his bluff.

Nick turned to look at her and frowned. 'You'd like that, wouldn't you? To get rid of me.'

'I spent a lot of time bringing you back to life on the last occasion you went swimming,' Sara reminded him evenly. 'Looks as if I was wasting my time.'

'Oh, so it was you, was it?' Nick said menacingly. 'Well, you needn't think I'm going to thank you, because. . .'

His eyes had moved to a spot behind her head and his expression changed.

'Hi, Dr Stephens. About time you came to see me. Where have you been for the last few days? Nobody seemed to know, and that woman doctor of yours said. . .'

'I hope you've been behaving yourself, Nick,' Chris Stephens said amiably. 'Not been giving you any trouble, I hope, Sister?'

Sara wheeled around to look at her errant boss. He was smiling and looking relaxed, although his safari suit was crumpled and damp with sweat, and she noticed the lines of fatigue around his dark brown eyes. There was mud on his shoes as if he'd come straight from the road to the clinic.

'Nick has been his usual self,' Sara said evenly. 'I think he'd like to have a chat with you about his medication. Let me know what you decide. I'll be in my office if you need me.'

'Hey, not so fast!' exclaimed Chris, putting out his arm as if to bar her escape. 'I'm going to need some help here. I've just had a long, tiring journey.'

'I'm on duty here,' Staff Nurse Preston put in hastily. 'Sister had just come along at my request to help me out with a difficult problem.'

'Then you're relieved of your duty for half an hour, Staff Nurse, because I want a word with Sister here. Go and get yourself a coffee, Molly. Now, Sister. . .'

He was looking down at her, an enigmatic smile on his handsome face.

Sara remained quite still, willing herself to feel calm. She heard the door closing as Molly Preston went out. Nick Cramer was looking from one to the other of them, his face clouded as he struggled to make sense of the situation.

'I think, Nick, that you and I had better have a little chat,' Chris said evenly, sitting down on the edge of the bed and motioning Sara to do the same.

The patient leaned back in his chair by the window, his eyes narrowing warily.

'OK, fire away, Doc; I know my rights. You can't keep me here against my will, and. . .'

He stopped in mid-sentence as Chris strode over to the door and flung it wide open.

'I wouldn't dream of keeping you here, Nick,' Chris said in a hard tone. 'In fact, you're a constant drain on the clinic finances. I was only thinking this morning that I ought to get rid of some of my charity cases, so please feel free to go as soon as you're ready.'

Sara waited with bated breath. Surreptitiously she glanced at Chris, standing stony-faced by the door. She hoped he was bluffing; it would be such a shame if their patient decided to leave. She wanted to see this case through to a successful conclusion. She had come to feel compassion for this unfortunate young man. There must have been some deep unhappiness in his life that led him to waste it like this.

'Well, if you don't want me here, if I'm a burden to you. . .' Nick began uncertainly, standing up and moving towards Sara.

'You're only a burden when you won't co-operate with the staff who give you your medical treatment,' Chris said quietly.

He remained by the door, watching his patient.

Nick moved to stand beside Sara. 'I suppose I should have thanked you for saving my life, Sister,' he said in a wavering tone, his eyes downcast. 'You weren't to know I wanted to end it all.'

'Now you're getting morbid again,' Chris said briskly. 'I'm not surprised, cooped up in this room. Either pack your bag and set off again on your travels or come out into the garden with us. We could all go for a swim in the pool. Have you tried the pool yet, Nick?'

The young man's eyes flickered. 'No. I haven't been swimming since. . .since that day down on the beach.'

'Oh, you'll love the pool,' Chris said quickly. He glanced at Sara. 'Get your bikini, Sister, and we'll have a quick dip. Molly Preston will be back soon.'

He moved quickly and took hold of Sara's hand, steering her towards the door. 'Keep moving,' he whispered as they went out.

They were halfway down the corridor before they heard the welcome shout from their patient.

'Hey, wait for me!'

Sara looked up at Chris and gave a sigh of relief. 'It worked,' she said quietly.

Chris smiled down at her, and she felt an uncertain melting feeling in the pit of her stomach.

'Of course it worked. Don't you trust me?'

She looked away. 'I wish I could,' she said.

The clinic swimming pool was surrounded by lush green bushes and multi-coloured tropical flowers. Carved out of stone, it gave the impression that it was part of a Balinese temple.

Sara remarked on this fact as she swam beside Chris. They were keeping an unobtrusive eye on Nick as he swam close by.

'That was the impression I was aiming for,' Chris told her. 'Bali is such a beautiful island. I didn't want to build anything that wouldn't blend in with the surroundings.'

'It must have been expensive to build this place,' she said, hauling herself on to the stone seat that was partly submerged at the side of the pool as she surveyed the small, luxurious kingdom that Chris had created. It was a world apart from the dusty, shabby streets beyond the high stone wall, and the swimming pool, set in the middle of the exotic gardens, was like an oasis of calm for patients and staff.

Chris pulled himself half out of the water on to the semi-submerged stone seat, playfully shaking drops all over Sara so that she had to push him away from her. He continued to splash his feet as he talked.

'You're obsessed by finance,' he said evenly. 'Why the fascination?'

She pulled her legs up to her chin, suddenly extremely aware of Chris's hard, muscular body so close to her own. Her bikini seemed skimpy. It was lunchtime, and there was no one else in the pool area except their patient, who was oblivious to them as he struck out in an energetic crawl, having obviously rediscovered his love of swimming. She felt terribly vulnerable as her eyes met Chris's.

'I'm not fascinated by money,' she explained carefully. 'It's the lack of it that worries me. I can't forget the awful feeling of helplessness when you can't pay the bills.'

'Were you poor when you were a child?' he asked gently.

She shook her head. 'No, I'm not talking about childhood. My parents were comfortably off.'

'So you were hard up after you got married?' he persisted. 'Didn't your parents offer to help you out?'

Sara leaned back against the warm stones, propping herself up on her elbows as she looked across at the ornamental gargoyle heads gushing water out into the clear blue pool. She reflected that the cost of one of the gargoyles would have paid Mike's monthly tobacconist bill, and then she wondered fleetingly if there were any more of his bills still outstanding that might arrive. Even three years on there were still people he owed money to, but she had left a forwarding address here in Bali.

'My parents would have offered help if I'd asked them,' she assured him. 'But I didn't tell them about my problems. They're retired and living in Florida now. They've both worked hard all their lives, and I didn't want to spoil their retirement. My brother and his wife and children live near my parents in Florida, and they all have a very pleasant life out there. I haven't seen them since before I was married.'

'Didn't they come to your wedding?' Chris asked in a surprised tone.

She gave a rueful smile. 'No; you see we got married in Gibraltar when we were on holiday. We just went over the border from Spain, taking our passports, and that was that.'

'Sounds very romantic,' remarked Chris.

Sara felt the sadness creeping over her again. 'Oh, it was. Mike swept me off my feet. I was on holiday with a couple of girl friends from hospital. Mike was staying in the same hotel, and he seemed such fun to be with. I enjoyed his impulsive behaviour. I'd never met anyone like him before. And I felt as if I'd known him all my life. . .'

Her voice trailed away as she looked up into Chris's eyes. She had had the same feeling for Chris as he'd held her in his arms on Kuta Beach in the moonlight.

'So when he proposed you accepted?' he prompted. 'Was that what happened?'

Sara nodded. 'I know it sounds naïve, but both my girl friends said I'd be mad to turn him down. They thought he was wonderful, and they told me how lucky I was to have made the perfect match. It looked like a once-in-a-lifetime romance. And he had so many friends out there in Spain; he was terribly popular. . . the life and soul of the party everywhere he went. I had no doubts about. . .'

Her voice trailed away as the memories came flooding back.

'With hindsight, I can see it was a simple holiday romance that should have been allowed to fizzle out . . .but I was besotted by him. I'd had such a careful, sheltered upbringing, and he introduced me to a whole new sophisticated world. The only thing was that Mike couldn't afford the lifestyle he hankered after. I went back to hospital and kept on my job, which was often the only support we had.'

'What was Mike's job?' asked Chris.

Sara hesitated. 'He was in the import-export business.'

He leaned back against the stones, his skin only inches from hers. The sun was directly above them, its fierce rays at their most dangerous in the middle of the day.

'We should go back into the shade,' Sara said, half rising. 'Nick's keeping cool as he swims, but. . .'

'Stay a moment longer,' Chris said huskily, his hand brushing her cheek, turning it so that she had to look straight into his eyes. 'I'm glad I know all about you now. It helps me to understand you.'

She looked into his dark, mysterious eyes and thought about all the things she hadn't told him. All the little details that would remain secret. She had only skimmed the surface of her previous life. There was so much that she didn't want to disclose to anyone. . .and especially to Chris.

Like it or not, she couldn't help feeling the sensuous rapport that was building up between them. But wasn't this just a case of history repeating itself? Was she doomed to make the same mistake a second time. . . falling for a man who was not what he seemed?

She moved away. There was no way of knowing. Her intuitions had been wrong first time around, and she didn't want to make the same mistake again.

Chris leaned across and put his bare hands on her shoulders. Slowly his lips came down on hers in a strong, sensuous, disturbing kiss.

'I want you to be happy here, Sara,' he told her in a husky voice.

She looked up into his eyes and knew that she hadn't felt so happy since those first few days with Mike. . . but how long could this last?

CHAPTER FIVE

FOR the next couple of weeks Chris remained at the Lotus Clinic, and Sara had more time to get to know him professionally. On the surface, he seemed to be a very caring and skilled doctor, always available to help her out when she had a problem to discuss.

But in many ways she found him to be a split personality. The carefree attitude he affected when they were out together during their off-duty time belied the sensitive nature he could display when they were treating a patient.

He continued to take her out on the town in the late evenings whenever they were both free together. She looked forward to this escape from their medical world, to the comparative cool of the night, the sound of the sea swishing on to the beach, the moonlight, and maybe a final swim in the Lotus pool.

As she gave her patient, Nick Cramer, his Methadone tablet she found her mind turning to the idyllic late-night swim she had had with Chris the previous evening. She knew Nick had been spending hours in the pool since she and Chris had reintroduced swimming into his life, and she could see a distinct improvement in his behaviour. Chris had reduced the Methadone dosage, and Nick hadn't complained.

She turned away from her patient now at the sound

of Chris's footsteps coming through the open door and smiled up at him.

'Nick's turning into a model patient,' she told him.

'I'm glad to hear it,' Chris said amiably. 'Because I've got a proposition to make.'

The patient swallowed the tablet and put down his glass of water. His eyes had taken on a guarded expression.

'I think it's time we thought about taking you completely off drugs, Nick,' Chris told him in a sympathetic tone.

The young man shook his head vigorously. 'Sorry, Doc, no chance! They've already tried to cure me back home and failed. I can't do without something to keep me together. I just fall apart if I don't get something.'

'But would you *like* to be able to do without drugs?' Chris asked gently.

'Well, of course I would!'

'Then that's half the battle over with,' said Chris. 'As long as you want to come off drugs we can help you. Now, what I'm proposing is that we give you a change of scenery. That always helps. I've got a clinic in the hills to the north of here at Ubud. It's quieter, more rural and peaceful. I think it will be easier for you to kick the habit up there. What do you say?'

Nick frowned. 'I don't know. It's nice here.' He glanced at Sara. 'I like the staff and I've got used to them. And I'd miss the swimming pool if. . .'

'There's a pool at my Ubud clinic,' Chris put in quickly. 'And Sister Freeman will be going along with you.'

Sara looked at him in surprise. This was the first she

had heard of the suggestion, but she wasn't going to question him in front of the patient. Knowing Chris, he had probably just dreamed up the scheme on the spur of the moment.

'Well, maybe,' the young man said uncertainly. 'I'll let you know.'

'Don't take too long,' Chris told him. 'I've got a long waiting list up there and I can only offer you the place today. Take it or leave it.'

Nick frowned. 'I don't like being rushed into things, but if you're sure Sister Freeman will be going with me. . .'

'Of course she will—won't you, Sister?' said Chris, a winning smile on his handsome face.

Sara swallowed hard. She liked her job here at the Lotus, and she didn't want to leave it for another leap into the unknown. It was too bad of Chris to put her on the spot like this. But it was just the sort of situation she had become used to. And if she didn't rise to the occasion now, all the hard work she had put in with this patient would be wasted.

'Who will be in charge of the nursing staff here at the Lotus if I go to Ubud?' she asked.

'Temporarily, I'll have to promote Staff Nurse Preston,' Chris told her. 'I've been impressed with her work ever since she came here. She was one of the applicants for your job, and I know she was disappointed when she didn't get it.'

There was silence in the room, broken only by the sound of the air-conditioning. Sara could feel her heart beating just a little too quickly. She was annoyed with Chris for moving her in what seemed like a demotion.

The Ubud Clinic would surely not be so prestigious as this one. But also at the back of her mind was the fear that she wouldn't see so much of Chris, that she would miss their off-duty time together.

Chris put out his hand and touched her arm. 'Well, what do you say?'

She was aware of the impatience in his eyes and of their young patient looking at her beseechingly.

'There's very little I can say,' she replied carefully. 'If you both want me to go to Ubud, then I'll go, but I insist on returning here just as soon as Nick's treatment is finished.'

The relief in Chris's eyes was patently obvious. He gave her a broad, thankful smile. 'You won't regret going to Ubud...and of course you can return here just as soon as Nick doesn't need you. And Molly Preston will hand back the reins. Now, isn't it time you were going for your swim, Nick?'

The young man smiled. 'I'm on my way!' He paused at the door. 'And thanks, Sister. I won't let you down.'

The door closed behind him and Sara was left alone with Chris.

'You might have discussed it with me,' she said crossly. 'Just when I was getting used to this place!'

He gave her a disarming smile. 'It seemed such a good idea. I wanted to strike while the iron was hot. And I know it will work out.' His face became serious again. 'Nick is an important patient to me. I want to try out the cold turkey technique on him. It will only work on selected patients, and we must have their complete co-operation. Nick trusts you implicitly, Sara, so I can't leave you out of this.'

'Cold turkey?' she queried. 'You mean stop all drugs and give nothing to replace them?'

'Exactly. It will mean six or seven unpleasant days for Nick. . .for everyone caring for him, until the withdrawal symptoms stop, but in the long run this is the best treatment for him. He's tried everything else. He wants to stop, which is half the battle. But he's going to need all the help he can get from both of us.'

'Both of us?' she repeated, feeling her pulses race just a little bit faster. 'You mean you're going to be there too?'

He hesitated, his eyes veiled and cautious. 'I shall try to be there. . .for some of the time, Sara. But, sometimes, as you know, I get called away urgently. . .'

'I know,' she said in a resigned tone. 'I know, only too well.'

He bent down and kissed her lightly on the cheek. 'How about dinner tonight? Your last night in Kuta.'

She took a deep breath. 'Ah, so I leave tomorrow, do I?'

He nodded. 'At the crack of dawn, before it gets hot on the road. I'll drive you and Nick up there. . .and then I'll have to go away for a few days. So we'll go out to dinner tonight to celebrate.'

'Celebrate what?' she asked in a bemused voice. Really, the man was incorrigible!

'Celebrate the imminent success with our patient,' he smiled. 'Or the fact that you've survived two months working for me without handing in your notice—or simply celebrate the fact that we're still friends.'

He put his hand under her chin and tilted her face so that she couldn't avoid his eyes.

'You're becoming very special to me, Sara,' he whispered.

She thought he would hear the beating of her heart as he looked down at her. Warning bells were ringing inside her head, but she found it hard to take notice. She realised, with absolute certainty, that she was falling hopelessly in love with this man. . .that he only had to lift his little finger and she would come running . . .that whatever he suggested she went along with. . . and she'd been down this road before. . .

'Why so solemn?' he asked gently.

Sara gave herself a mental shake and put on a bright smile.

'Is that better? Do you like me to be happy all the time?'

'That's much better. That's the mental image I take with me when I have to go away. An attractive, smiling face, not classically beautiful, a little thin, perhaps, but instantly lovely when you light it up with that indefinable inner glow of happiness. . .and a lovely wide, sensuous mouth, made to be kissed. . .'

His lips were swift and feather-light as they melted against hers.

'Careful, someone might come in!' she remonstrated laughingly, pulling herself away and straightening her frilly sister's cap. 'You're so impulsive!'

Chris smiled. 'I know. But that's the way you affect me.'

For an instant she had the distinct impression that he was mocking her. She doubted his sincerity. . .she doubted so many things about him.

But she couldn't help the way she felt about him. . .

that deep insatiable hunger inside her that longed for real love.

'So we have a date for tonight,' he said breezily. 'I'll come round for a drink about eight.'

As the sun went down so the temperature reduced to something bearable. Sara sat out on her patio, the doors of her cottage closed to keep in the cool air-conditioned atmosphere for her return from a night on the town with Chris.

She poured him a beer as soon as he arrived. She drank only fruit juice. For this last evening she wanted to keep her wits about her.

She had had a busy day sorting out the administration hand-over to Molly Preston. The staff nurse had been delighted to be promoted to sister. Sara had no qualms about the arrangement—she knew that her colleague would cope well with the extra responsibility. But she felt a certain sadness at leaving the Lotus Clinic.

'You know, I've come to think of this place as home,' she told Chris. 'I'll be glad when it's time to come back here.'

He smiled. 'You may find you prefer to stay in Ubud. You haven't seen what you're in for yet, so you should reserve judgement. I can make my home anywhere. . .wherever I lay my head, as the song says.'

'Don't you have a permanent home?' she asked, realising that she knew nothing of Chris's background.

His eyes flickered momentarily. 'I did have a permanent home. . .once,' he said, in a faraway voice.

'But it was all a long time ago. . .and I prefer to move around. Footloose and fancy free, that's me.'

'So I've noticed,' she said.

'He jumped up. 'Time to go. I'm starving.'

He drove them through the narrow streets to a beachside restaurant. Sara looked out across the darkened sea, lit only by the lights from the boats moored by the shore. Above her, the neon sign from the restaurant illuminated the sandy road.

They had a delicious seafood cocktail of prawns and crab, followed by succulent roast chicken with fresh asparagus. The music was subdued and they were able to talk easily. But however Sara tried, she couldn't steer the conversation around to Chris's home life again. Whenever personal questions were made, he ducked out and changed the subject.

Afterwards, they walked barefoot on the beach, savouring the nocturnal breeze that had sprung up, even though it was blowing some of the sand around.

'I'm going to miss the sea,' said Sara, dipping her bare foot into the still-warm water.

'You'll love the hills,' Chris whispered, taking her gently into his arms.

She relaxed against him as he kissed her, knowing that she would love anywhere if Chris was there with her. It was all too good to be true. . .like the last time she had fallen in love.

'Time to go back,' he said gently, as he released her from his arms. 'We've got to leave at sunrise.'

She felt the excited tingling of her whole body, the delicious sensual arousal deep inside her, and she wanted the night to go on forever.

But when they returned, Chris seemed anxious to get away.

Just as well, Sara thought as she went alone into the welcoming cool of her cottage. She knew she was reaching the point of no return—the point at which she had to decide how much of herself she should commit to this disturbingly attractive man. She had to find out more about him...as she should have done last time.

The sun was barely warming the hibiscus at the side of the patio as she emerged next morning clad in cotton trousers and shirt, her feet encased in open sandals.

Chris was waiting for her in the reception area having already been to collect their patient. Nick looked uncharacteristically well-groomed, having had his beard trimmed and his hair cut.

'Didn't recognise you, Nick,' Sara quipped.

'Neither did I,' smiled Chris.

There was a rustle of clothing behind them and they both turned to watch Dr Cassandra coming in. She paused in the doorway to adjust her sari.

Sara couldn't help thinking that the doctor looked prettier when she wasn't wearing European dress. The Indian side of her parentage was very prominent, and the colourful saris she wore early in the morning or in her off-duty time were very becoming.

Chris moved forward to greet his colleague. 'It's good of you to come and see us off, Cassandra,' he smiled. 'I hope you won't have any problems while I'm away.'

Dr Cassandra smiled serenely. 'There won't be anything I can't handle, Chris. I've spent a lot of time in charge here, if you remember.'

'You're invaluable, Cassandra,' Chris told her.

His colleague didn't reply, but the serene smile expanded and Sara had the distinct impression that the woman doctor was well aware of how indispensable she was.

'Well, come along, we'd better get this show on the road,' Chris said breezily.

'I shall look forward to your return,' Dr Cassandra told him.

The early morning streets of Kuta were surprisingly busy. The small cafés were opening up their shutters, and the smell of freshly baked bread wafted out invitingly, reminding Sara that she hadn't had time for breakfast.

The narrow streets gave way to a broad highway and then a dusty road that carved its way through green rice fields where the people were already at work, their heads covered with straw cloche-like hats ready to protect them from the increasing heat of the sun. Palm-leaf scarecrows were dotted around the countryside, and many of the fields had shrines and small temples honouring the deities of agriculture who were supposed to give their blessing to the harvest.

They reached the small village of Peliatan on the outskirts of Ubud by mid-morning. Chris slowed down the Land Rover and pulled to a stop so that they could watch some dancers in a courtyard beside the road. Sara found herself fascinated by the spectacle. She eased herself out of her seat and moved over the uneven stone pavement to get a better view.

Chris followed her, bringing Nick with him so that he could explain what was happening.

'The dance tradition is very strong around here,' he began as they settled themselves in a good position for viewing in the shade of a tall palm tree. 'That man is an instructor who's showing the steps to those three young girls. They try to imitate all his steps and movements exactly. I think they're rehearsing for a performance of the *legong*, one of the classical Balinese dances which depicts one of their mythical legends.'

'They're very young, aren't they?' Sara whispered.

Chris smiled down at her. 'They start their dancing training when they're about five. These girls are probably seven or eight and obviously skilled enough to perform in public. Dancers of this kind are considered over the hill at fourteen.'

Sara's eyes widened in surprise. 'Then I won't try to join in. I'll stick to nursing.'

He put his hand loosely on her shoulder. 'Good thinking! You're more use to me as a nurse than a dancer. . . Look, have you noticed how beautiful their costumes are?'

Sara nodded as she admired the tiny figures tightly bound in gold brocade, their heads crowned with frangipani blossoms.

'It must be very difficult to move in those garments,' she said. 'They must be suffocating in this heat.'

'That's all part of the training,' Chris told her. 'They have to dance like divine nymphs and act out various aspects of the legend. The *legong* dance is about a wicked king who was warned by a bird of ill omen not to go to battle, but he took no notice.'

'And what happened?' Nick had been listening to Chris's explanation with interest.

'I think the king came to a bad end but, as nobody liked him, the audience won't be too disturbed,' Chris told him.

Sara felt glad that Nick was actually taking an interest in the dancing. Some of his bored veneer was gradually chipping away.

The young girls made a beautiful sight as they moved gracefully in the sunlight to the beat of the drum and the music of a xylophone played by a young man swathed in colourful cotton.

'Ubud and its surrounding area is rich in culture,' Chris continued. 'As well as a strong musical tradition there are many artists living out here. You must visit some of the galleries and see the paintings and works of art.'

'I'd like that,' said Nick.

Sara and Chris turned to look at their patient and then their eyes met in approval. They had been pleased that he had taken to swimming again, but it would be a major achievement if he started to take an interest in the arts.

'I used to paint,' Nick went on. 'I had an exhibition once in London. . .nothing very grand. It was after I left art school, and a few of us got together and rented a studio where we could show our stuff. . .'

He stopped, apparently embarrassed that he had their undivided attention.

'Like I said, nothing very grand,' he finished.

Sara put her hand on his arm. 'Why don't we go and buy some paints in Ubud? You could get started while you're out here with time on your hands.'

Nick began to shake visibly and he put his hand to his stomach. 'I don't think so. . .not yet. The cramps are coming back. Can you give me something, quick?'

Chris gave a barely perceptible nod, and Sara delved inside her bag for the bottle of Methadone. As she handed over one of the tablets she thought to herself that she wasn't going to give up on this one. Her patient had shown a creative side she hadn't dreamed of, and she was going to pursue this. If she could give Nick a real reason for wanting to live, the drug habit could become a thing of the past.

They had to reluctantly leave the dancing rehearsal in full flow because Chris wanted to get to the clinic. Sara found she was apprehensive at the prospect of arriving at her temporary home.

The entrance to the clinic at the side of a long narrow road away from the centre of the town was unprepossessing, but as soon as they drove through the gateway she felt her spirits lift.

A large sign proclaimed that they had arrived at the Temple Clinic. And indeed the theme of the temple was carried right the way through the buildings. The central administrative area was ornately carved and decorated, but it was the surrounding medical units that were the most picturesque. They had been built in the style of small wooden temples, brightly coloured, with wooden or stone statues on their verandahs. Multi-coloured tiles led from the outside areas through to the vast, high-ceilinged rooms cooled by enormous fans set in the roof.

Sara looked around her in amazement.

'It must have been some feat to build this place,' she said to Chris. 'Part of it looks as if it's been carved out of a ravine. That part over there, for example. . .the rugged section that's sloping down to the river. However did they manage to construct that house?'

Chris laughed. 'With great difficulty. But that's how I wanted it. Let's go and take a look. It's my house, but there's plenty of room. Would you like to share it with me?'

Her pulses raced. 'How do you mean. . .share it with you?' she asked warily.

He smiled. 'Oh, nothing improper, I assure you, Sister! There are lots of rooms. You can have your own large bedroom, sitting-room and bathroom. And you'll have the place to yourself for most of the time when I'm away. But when I'm here we can share the main downstairs room that opens out on to the veranda. That way we can have long discussions about our patients. I'll be able to catch up on medical reports with you, and the staff will know where to find us in an emergency and. . .look, do I need to go on justifying the situation?'

He held out his hand. 'Come and look at the place. You'll love it.'

She was sure she would, if only she could stop the warning bells from ringing in her head.

CHAPTER SIX

CHRIS was right. Sara loved the large wooden house at the edge of the ravine, from the very first moment she set foot on the wide veranda that ran around it.

The east-facing veranda, now bathed in morning sunlight, had large wooden pillars supporting the bamboo roofing. The tiled floor was still relatively cool because of the shade. She kicked off her sandals and walked across it barefoot, revelling in the feeling of freedom it gave her.

She touched one of the two grey stone elephants covered with cloth saddles that guarded the wide-open entrances to the house as if they belonged to an ancient temple. Their long trunks had been carved in a swirling motion that pointed towards the ground and their necks were embellished with golden beads.

A bamboo table was placed between two of the pillars, and it was flanked by a long wooden sofa covered in batik cotton.

'Let's have breakfast before we look at the rest of the house,' said Chris, sitting down on the sofa and inviting Sara to join him. 'I'm starving, and I'm sure you are.'

Her hunger had temporarily disappeared in the excitement of arriving at this fascinating place, but it returned as soon as she saw the food set out on a tray.

A young servant boy came out of the house carrying it on his head.

She held her breath until the boy had set the tray down on the table.

Chris poured out hot coffee while the houseboy served hot rolls, jam and butter.

'I hope Nick's being well taken care of,' said Sara, as she took a sip of her orange juice. It was freshly squeezed and tasted delicious.

'Don't worry,' Chris told her. 'Dr Astuti is an experienced man. He especially wanted to examine Nick and settle him into his room before conferring with us. He likes to make his own observations about patients.'

'Even so, however well qualified Dr Astuti is, there's nothing like the personal touch,' Sara said. 'Nick is used to us and I hope he won't think we've temporarily abandoned him. I must say, though, I did like the look of our Indonesian doctor. He seems very kind,' she added, remembering the pleasant manner the doctor had when they were introduced soon after their arrival.

She had learned that Dr Astuti was in charge of the Temple Clinic in Chris's absence.

'You can go and see Nick when I've shown you around the house,' Chris told her. 'Perhaps we'd better start now, because I don't have too much time.'

She felt a sudden pang of disappointment. 'Are you leaving immediately?' she asked.

His eyes flickered momentarily as he faced her. 'Afraid so.'

She took a deep breath. 'Would you mind telling me where you're going?'

He hesitated. 'You don't need to worry about where I'm going. You'll be fully occupied here, and Dr Astuti will look after you.'

'Is it some kind of medical emergency?' she persisted, feeling she had a right to know what Chris was up to.

His eyes took on a veiled, enigmatic expression. 'Something like that,' he agreed, as he stood up. 'Look, I really think we should be making a move. Let me show you around the house. Like I said, you'll love it.'

She certainly did love it, as she went from room to room, marvelling at the high ceilings, the ornamental carvings of wood and stone, the bronze figures depicting legendary deities and the comfortable bamboo furniture liberally scattered with soft, brightly coloured cushions. There were tropical flowers in every room, obviously fresh from the garden that morning.

But it was her own little domain that was the most appealing part of the house. Completely self-contained on the first floor at the top of a wide wooden staircase was an airy sitting-room perfumed by numerous vases of flowers, cooled by a large ceiling fan, with such an inviting feeling about the place that she wanted to claim it immediately. The bedroom which led off from it was no less welcoming, with its cool cotton-sheeted bed and ornately carved dressing-table.

She went through the door beside the bed to the bathroom. It was simple but clean; there was a white newly scrubbed bath and a basin with a tiny mirror.

She spun round, having seen Chris's reflection in the mirror. He was leaning against the doorpost, a bemused smile on his handsome face.

'So is Madame satisfied with her accommodation?' he asked in a benign voice. 'Is she quite sure that my intentions are completely honourable?'

'Oh, Chris, it's lovely!'

On the spur of the moment, she went towards him, putting her arms up on to his shoulders.

His hands swooped to her waist and he held her in a firm grip. She looked up into his eyes and saw real tenderness. . .and something else. Yes, she was sure she could see her own growing love mirrored in those dark pools. Maybe her suspicions were unfounded. . . maybe she should trust this man implicitly. . .

His lips had found hers in a tender, satisfying kiss. She abandoned herself to the moment, leaving all rational thoughts behind her. There would be more of these idyllic moments here in this warm friendly house, and she knew she would live through each one as if there were no tomorrow.

It was Chris who pulled himself away and held her at arm's length.

'I have to go,' he said huskily. 'I don't even have time to show you around the clinic. I'll ask Dr Astuti.'

He was already turning away, moving through her little domain with a purposeful step.

'When will you be back?' she asked as he reached the outer door of her sitting-room.

He turned, and she saw the look of impatience on his face as he replied, 'I really couldn't say. Dr Astuti will be in charge. Goodbye, Sara.'

She remained standing motionless after Chris had gone, feeling the cooling of the fan on her upturned face. She had a tremendous feeling of déjà vu. How many times in her life had she waited for the man in her life to return, not knowing where he was, not knowing what he was up to?

She gave herself a mental shake. She had never allowed herself to be defeated by that situation and she wasn't about to let it happen now. There was always work to be done. How thankful she was that she had her nursing training to make sense of her complicated life. When she was with her patients she didn't have time to worry about herself.

She stripped off her travel-soiled clothes and had a quick dip in the tiny bathtub. Refreshed, she put on the clean uniform that had been laid out on her bed by some unseen hands while she bathed. It appeared that the house had a full complement of Indonesian servants, ever watchful and ready to help, but going quietly away when they were not required. One of them must have brought up her luggage.

As she fixed her cap in front of the tiny dressing-table mirror she reflected that it was a good thing she had decided to stay in this house. She could easily have decided against it when they first arrived. But from the look of all the preparations it seemed as if everyone had expected her to settle in here. Chris must have been pretty sure of himself when he gave the instructions to his staff!

She found Dr Astuti taking down Nick's case history, and from the reams of notes he was making it appeared that he had got more information out of the young man than Sara and Chris had.

Her patient looked up when she went into his room and smiled with relief.

'Do you think I could have a break from all this interrogation, Sister?' asked Nick, deliberately avoiding Dr Astuti's eyes. 'I could do with a swim. Dr Stephens said there was a pool here.'

Sara glanced at her colleague. 'I'm sure you could spare Nick for a short time, couldn't you, Dr Astuti? We had an early start today and he's probably feeling tired.'

The Indonesian doctor smiled and nodded. 'But of course, Sister Freeman. I'll finish this later.' He turned to look at his patient. 'Run along, young man. You'll find everything you need down at the pool. There are a couple of nurses always in attendance, both of them excellent lifesavers.'

'I don't need a lifesaver,' Nick began. He broke off and gave Sara a wry grin. 'Well, not usually!'

Sara smiled at her patient. 'Go and enjoy yourself. I'll see you when you get back.'

She was fully occupied for the rest of the day, finding her way around the clinic and settling into the work. Dr Astuti showed her the different departments that were spread over the entire area of the clinic gardens, each in its own temple-like house.

On her return to the reception area she met the sister-in-charge, a charming Indonesian woman of about forty.

Sister Ida Poleng was quick to point out that she recognised that Sara would only be working at the Temple Clinic in a temporary capacity. She knew that Sara was the sister-in-charge at the Lotus Clinic, and she didn't want her to feel demoted. Dr Stephens, it appeared, had made it quite clear that both sisters were on equal footing in the hierarchy.

But Sister Poleng, smiling in her charming way, explained that she would continue to organise the nursing staff. There was a higher proportion of Indonesian nurses in the Temple Clinic and many of them had only basic English. Consequently she conversed with them in their own language.

She added that if Sister Freeman would take on the bulk of the work with the ever-increasing influx of tourist patients she would be most relieved. The vast majority of the tourists were English-speaking, and they welcomed the chance of being cared for by an English sister.

Sara assured her Indonesian colleague that she would be happy to comply with her wishes, and, when asked when she would like to start, she replied that she was ready at once. She knew there was nothing she wanted more than to get on with her medical work and forget the man who threatened to turn her world upside down.

The medical unit where many of the tourists were treated was in a house close to the swimming pool. Aptly nicknamed the Holiday Camp by some of the Australian nurses, it had all the trappings of a luxury hotel.

'Some of the patients don't want to leave,' Staff Nurse Vanessa Williams told Sara as she showed her around the large airy building. 'They come along to our morning surgery sessions complaining of diarrhoea. We put them on Lomotil or Imodium and tell them to stick to a diet of hot tea for a couple of days. If they're still suffering after forty-eight hours we advise them to return for further tests. They always ask if they can have a look around the place, and they're so impressed they start enquiring how much it would cost to spend a few days being treated as an in-patient. Dr Stephens has set a special rate for those cases. He doesn't really want to fill up the beds with non-emergencies. But if we've got spare beds and these patients are willing to pay and begging to be admitted, we take them.'

They were standing by an upstairs window looking down on the swimming pool.

Sara smiled. 'They look very happy to me.' Her eyes caught a movement under one of the nearby poolside umbrellas. She could see Nick Cramer stretched out on a chaise-longue, looking up at one of the Indonesian nurses, a particularly pretty girl wearing a short white cotton dress with a becoming cap perched on the top of her shiny dark hair. There was something about the expression on Nick's face that gave Sara a start.

There was a definitely provocative expression on her patient's face, and the young nurse was obviously enjoying their conversation. The older nurse on duty by the pool was coming across. Sara noticed the impatient words that were exchanged between the two nurses and the reluctance with which the young nurse moved away, giving Nick a sideways, conspiratorial glance as she left.

Now that would be a help, Sara found herself thinking. A spot of romance in Nick's life would be a distinct advantage when they started the cold turkey treatment.

The very thought of it made her break out in imaginary shivers. She remembered treating drugs patients in London during her training, and it had been most unpleasant for everyone involved.

She turned to look at the staff nurse beside her. 'Thanks, Nurse. I'll carry on by myself from here. You've been a great help.'

The Australian smiled as she went back to her duties. Sara looked out across the pool to the hills brooding dark and mysterious in the background. Was that where Chris had gone?

Her one fear was that Chris was mixed up in something shady, some kind of activity that gave him the wealth he obviously had. Because she couldn't see any other way he could finance his projects. Even charging exorbitant prices to eager private patients wouldn't bring in the sort of revenue Chris required to build and maintain his luxury clinics.

And the most obvious means of making money out here in the Far East was drugs. Sara felt the awful cold realisation of her fear in the pit of her stomach. Could it be that Chris was actually involved with the drug barons on the one hand while he cared for the victims of the trade on the other? She hated herself for even allowing such a disloyal thought to enter her mind, but she had to consider the facts. . .and that was one thing she hadn't done when Mike had kept disappearing on strange assignments.

No, it hadn't occurred to her to consider that Mike's failing export and import business was being propped up by more sinister financial arrangements. It was only when the police had arrived on that fateful night to tell her Mike had been killed that the dreadful truth had come out.

She put her hands out to grip the wooden window-ledge as she felt once more the horror of realising the truth. But Chris was a doctor, committed to saving lives, not to ruining them. He couldn't split himself into two completely different characters, like Jekyll and Hyde—could he?

She jumped as someone put a hand on her shoulder. Turning around from the window, she found herself looking into the kindly face of Sister Poleng.

'I came to see if you would come along and help me with a newly admitted patient, Sister Freeman,' she said, in her softly lilting, heavily accented voice. 'It's a young English girl who's gone into premature labour, and she's very frightened.'

'But of course,' said Sara immediately, anxiously ridding her mind of the unwelcome thoughts.

CHAPTER SEVEN

WHEN Sara arrived at the obstetrics unit, a large airy building set well apart from the rest of the medical units, she found her patient, Fiona Brown, a young girl from London, in a highly emotional state. Fiona was seven months pregnant and on a delayed honeymoon with her twenty-year-old husband.

She seized hold of Sara's hand and held on for dear life. 'Don't leave me, Sister! I can't understand the other nurses—they don't listen to me. I can't have this baby yet. It's not due for another couple of months, and. . .'

'I understand, Fiona. Just leave everything to us,' Sara said in a soothing voice as she began her examination.

The birth canal was already widely dilated. Minimal preparations would have to be made. But first she had to soothe her distraught patient.

She was relieved to find an Entonox machine. Sister Poleng was already fixing it up. Sara moved it over to her patient and helped her to breathe into the soothing mask. Gradually the patient became a little calmer.

The young husband had begged to be allowed to go out into the gardens for some air. It was obvious to Sara that he wasn't going to be of any use to his wife during the labour.

Dr Astuti arrived, and together they scrubbed up

and donned sterile gowns and gloves. The birth was imminent; Sara could see the head. She held her patient's hand, urging her to pant.

'Don't push, Fiona,' she said gently. 'Save your strength. . . I'll tell you when. . .'

It was a very quick birth. The tiny premature girl weighed only four pounds. Sara wrapped the minute infant in a cotton dressing towel and hovered anxiously beside the new mother, who wanted to hold her daughter.

'Oh, she's so small, so crinkly-looking. . .like a little old lady. . .but very beautiful,' smiled Fiona, her weary face relaxing. 'She is going to be OK, isn't she, Sister?'

Sara assured her patient that the baby was in good hands, that all she had to do now was rest and get her strength back. The medical staff would do the rest.

Gently Sara lifted the baby into her arms and placed her in the waiting incubator. Then she wheeled the incubator away to the adjoining room that served as a nursery.

She found there were two other newborn babies, both Indonesian, both full term and obviously thriving, judging by the lusty cries that were coming from their cots. She knew her poor little English infant was going to require expert medical attention, and she would make sure that everything possible was done to care for her during the first few crucial days of her life.

Two weeks passed, during which Sara was kept extremely busy working with her premature infant and coping with the influx of tourist patients suffering from a variety of ailments. The work was absorbing and interesting, and it kept her from brooding about Chris. She thought about him at night and in her off-duty, but deliberately pushed him from her mind when she was working in the clinic.

But on a warm morning, as she bottle-fed her little English prem, she heard his voice out in the garden, and her heart started to pound with excitement. Two whole weeks since she'd seen him. . .no message, no phone call.

'Hello, Sara.' He was standing in the doorway, his face outlined in the sun.

She saw his travel-stained safari suit, his stubbly unshaven face, his dusty feet clad in even dustier sandals, but none of this registered in her mind. All she could see was the tender expression on his face as he looked down at her feeding the baby. And she decided that wherever he'd been, whatever he'd been up to, she didn't want to know. She wanted to remain ignorant of his activities so that she could go on loving him.

'Hello, Chris,' she said, in a voice that threatened to crack. 'When did you get back?'

'Just now. . . I came straight away to find you.'

'That was considerate of you.'

The feeding bottle was empty. Sara placed it on the cotside table and gently rubbed her little patient's back. There was a gratifying burp, and Sara smiled as she continued to stroke the baby soothingly.

'Good girl! Now I'm just going to change your nappy, and. . .'

'Is this the little English prem?' asked Chris, bending down to take the baby from Sara.

'Yes, this is Deborah Brown, daughter of Fiona and Tim. She shouldn't have put in an appearance for another couple of months. Fiona and Tim got married last year and have been saving up for the honeymoon of a lifetime. But they hadn't planned on having their baby with them.'

She realised she was talking too quickly, almost gabbling in her unaccustomed nervousness.

'She looks as if she's thriving.' Chris cast an expert eye over the baby. 'I'd like to give her a more thorough examination when I've cleaned up. How much does she weigh?'

Sara took the baby back into her arms, her hands unavoidably brushing against Chris's chest. She felt a fleeting sensual shiver run down her spine and turned away, still holding the baby so that he couldn't see her reaction.

'Deborah weighed four pounds at birth; she lost weight initially, but two weeks later she's gained half a pound on the birth weight. As soon as she's five pounds the parents will take her away. They're worrying about the cost of all this treatment. I think they'd like to see you about it as soon as possible.'

'Where are they?' Chris asked.

'They've moved out of their honeymoon hotel into a cheap *losmen* lodging house. Fiona had to spend a week here before she was strong enough to be allowed out.'

'Contact them and get them over here as soon as possible,' Chris told her. 'There's no problem with the finance—I'll sort something out for them. I don't want them worrying unnecessarily.'

Sara swallowed hard. 'I didn't think the finance would be a problem. In fact, I tried to tell them that. . .'

She stopped in mid-sentence, unprepared for the gleam of interest in Chris's eyes.

'You tried to tell them what?' he asked, his voice dangerously low.

'I tried to tell them that you were a generous person,' she finished hurriedly, deliberately averting her eyes. 'But they continued to worry. . .said they wouldn't believe it until they'd spoken to you.'

She bent over the baby girl, peeling off her nappy, gently cleansing the delicate skin before fixing a fresh nappy on. Her back was towards Chris and she didn't want to turn round to face him. She placed the baby in her cot and straightened up again.

She found that Chris was watching her with a strange, enigmatic expression as she turned round.

'I don't want you to interfere in the financial side of the clinic,' he said carefully, in a steely hard voice. 'I'm glad you tried to reassure the baby's parents, but be careful not to overstep the mark in future.'

Sara bit back the hasty retort that sprang to her lips. How dared he lecture her on the subject of finance! She who was scrupulously honest, when he. . .heaven knew what his moral values consisted of!

She realised that she was glaring at him; she took a deep breath. 'Will that be all?' she asked coldly.

He turned away. 'For the moment. I'll be back in an hour.'

She hoped she would feel calmer when he returned. Leaving her infant patient in the capable hands of the staff nurse, she went across to the medical unit to check on Nick Cramer.

'Nick's down by the pool, Sister,' Staff Nurse Vanessa Williams told her, with a knowing smile. 'He spends most of his time there now.'

'Has he had any Methadone this morning?' asked Sara.

'No, he said he wanted to get through the day without it,' was the encouraging reply.

Sara smiled. 'That's a step in the right direction. How about his evening medication?'

'Oh, he always insists on that. Says he can't sleep without it.'

Sara nodded thoughtfully. It was time they got on with the cold turkey treatment. She would speak to Chris about it when he returned.

She found Nick down by the pool, stretched out on a chaise-longue, just as she'd seen him that day she had looked out of the window and wondered if she was witnessing an impending romance between her patient and the young poolside nurse.

'Hello, Nick, what have you been up to lately?' she began. 'I've been so busy over in Obstetrics I haven't had much time for you.'

Nick smiled. 'That's all right. I've been well looked after, Sister.'

His eyes moved fondly towards the young Indonesian nurse who was walking towards him carrying a glass of mango juice tinkling with ice cubes.

'So I see,' smiled Sara. 'Don't you think it's time we considered giving you the treatment I discussed with you?'

'Good morning, Sister,' the young nurse said, giving a bright smile that displayed small white perfectly formed teeth.

Sara smiled back, thinking what an attractive girl the nurse was. No wonder Nick was so obviously besotted!

'Good morning, Nurse Ngurah,' she said. 'Are you enjoying your work with your patients here by the pool?'

'I like it very much,' Nurse Ngurah replied shyly.

'Thank you, Mai,' said Nick as he took the glass from the Indonesian nurse. He waited until she had moved away again.

'I don't think I'm ready for the full treatment yet, Sister,' he said carefully, taking a sip from his glass.

'But you don't know until you try!' Sara protested, a little more impatiently than she'd intended.

Nick stared at her. 'What's got into you today? That's the first time I've seen you lose your cool, Sister. What's the matter? Are you missing Dr Stephens?'

Sara looked at the grinning face and her patience almost snapped. She took a deep breath to steady herself. She would ignore the gibe. This was a patient who needed her full help and co-operation if he was to get well, and, she couldn't afford to lose her professional calm.

'As a matter of fact, Dr Stephens has returned, so I'll get him to have a word with you. The fact is, we can't keep you here indefinitely living in the lap of luxury without making a real attempt to kick the drugs.'

As she started to move away, she was aware of the worried expression on Nick's face. Maybe she should have continued the softly-softly approach a little longer. Perhaps she was being harsh on the poor lad. Oh, well, he was Chris's patient, and if she'd overstepped the mark again she would be for the high jump!

'I'll be in Obstetrics if you need me, Nick,' she finished, trying to sound more sympathetic. 'Remember, I'm always ready for a chat with you.'

When Chris returned to Obstetrics he found Sara feeding one of the Indonesian babies. He strode purposefully between the row of cots.

'Aren't you encouraging our mothers to breast-feed any more?' he asked testily.

She kept her eyes on the tiny infant. 'Of course we are. But this little one had a hard time getting into the world, and the mother needs a couple of days' rest. She's expressed this milk, as a matter of fact.'

'Oh. . . I'm sorry if I sounded sharp. I'm very tired—haven't had much sleep.'

She felt his hand on her shoulder and looked up into the deep brown, expressive eyes. She saw that he had shaved and obviously showered; his light brown wavy hair was still wet, still sticking to his forehead in unruly strands. But there were marks of strain and exhaustion on his handsome face. Her heart went out to him. If only he would confide in her. . .tell her his secrets. . . admit to her that his life wasn't as simple as he tried to make out in his over-confident manner.

'You should take some rest,' she told him gently.

'I'll rest when I've been round the hospital and taken up the reins again,' he told her. 'I want to examine little Deborah, and then I'll go to see Nick. How is he?'

'He's improving,' Sara replied guardedly. 'Go and see for yourself. I think it's time we started the full treatment, but he thinks otherwise.'

She finished feeding the infant, put him back in his cot and went over to help Chris examine baby Deborah.

Chris nodded in satisfaction at the end of the full examination. 'Excellent! In a few months our little prem will be as healthy as if she'd gone to full term. But I'd like to keep her in for a few weeks—the lungs are still immature, and I wouldn't fancy her chances out there with young inexperienced parents.'

'I hoped you'd say that,' Sara said. 'I've sent a message to the parents to come and see you this afternoon.'

'Fine. I'll go and see Nick first.' He paused in the doorway. 'Are you free this evening, Sara?'

'I could be.'

He smiled. 'Well, if you could be ready, say, about eight, we could go out for a meal.'

He went out through the open doorway, not looking back and not waiting for her reply.

So sure of himself! she thought. So confident of her reaction. Giving nothing away, but expecting too much from her. Wasn't it time she started to assert herself? Maybe Chris would value her confidence more if she remained cooler with him. Perhaps if he saw that he couldn't take her for granted he would share some of his secrets.

It was a long shot, but it was worth a try.

At the end of the long day she went back to her little domain and wrote a note for Chris which she gave to one of the houseboys with instructions to pass it on to the doctor as soon as he came off duty.

She was in the bathtub, her shoulders submerged in foam, when she heard the loud knocking on her outer door. She ignored it. It was no good shouting out from the bathroom; her voice wouldn't travel through the bedroom and the sitting-room.

She finished her bath, taking her time. The knocking on the door had been repeated once, but then the house had gone silent.

She thought about the note she'd written telling Chris she was too tired to go out. Had he received it yet, and was that him knocking on the door? Oh, she hoped so!

CHAPTER EIGHT

THE house was still and quiet when she padded back into her bedroom wrapped in a towel. She decided that Chris had got the message that she didn't want to be disturbed that evening. She couldn't help feeling disappointed that she was to spend her evening alone, but if it brought Chris to his senses it would have been worth it!

She lay down on her bed and flicked through one of the magazines she had brought with her from Kuta, but her mind wandered away from the pages so many times that she tossed it back on to her bedside table and stared up at the ceiling. A mosquito was flying near the light. She would have to get rid of it before she went to sleep.

She looked around her room and realised that the servants had omitted to light an anti-mosquito coil in her room. Perhaps that had been the houseboy bringing one up when she was in the bath.

She felt a pang of disillusion. So it hadn't been Chris after all! What a let-down. . .and she'd thought he was finding her indispensable already. He was probably sitting in the restaurant enjoying an excellent dinner, not giving her a thought.

There was nothing for it except to go downstairs and arrange for a coil to be lit in her room. She stood up and wrapped herself in the cotton sarong she'd bought in Kuta. It was the most useful garment she had for off-duty time in the house. It was cool, comfortable and easy to slip in and out of.

She padded barefoot down the stairs and made for the kitchen. The young houseboy was closing up the windows for the night and he turned and smiled at Sara.

'I came to bring you a lighted coil, but. . .' he began.

'I'm sorry—I was in the bath,' Sara explained.

'I will take it up now.'

'Thank you.' She moved outside the kitchen, suddenly feeling restless. She was probably wasting her evening for nothing.

She sat down on one of the bamboo chairs, listening to the night sounds all around her. The croaking of the frogs was growing louder. It was like a chorus of old men enlivened by the occasional high-pitched soprano of the cicadas.

She needed some air before she slept. It felt hot in the house with the windows closed, even though the fan still whirred around above her.

She walked barefoot across the polished floor and out on to the veranda.

'I got your note.'

She jumped at the unexpected sound of Chris's voice, and her heart gave a double turn. He was sitting on the veranda beside one of the low bamboo tables, a glass of whisky in his hand.

'I didn't know you were here,' she began. 'I thought you would have gone out for a meal.'

'That was the original plan, but when you opted out I rang up and cancelled the table.'

'Oh. . . I'm sorry.'

'It doesn't matter—I was tired too. Would you like a drink, or are you going to bed?'

She felt his eyes sweeping appreciatively over her sarong, lingering on her bare shoulders. And she knew she wanted to be with him this evening. . .she'd missed him so much. Playing hard to get didn't seem to be working!

'I'd like a gin and tonic,' she said as she sat down at the other side of the table from him.

Chris got up and went into the house. Moments later he returned with the houseboy, who was carrying a drinks tray.

Sara lay back in her chair, sipping her drink and absorbing the calming atmosphere of the tropical night. It was still warm, but not oppressively so.

'This is the best part of the day,' Chris said quietly.

'Yes, I've come to realise that in the short time I've been here. There's something magical about the nights out here. When the sun has gone down everything seems different. It's like a completely new world. . .a world where we don't have any cares. I find it easy to relax after sundown in the tropics, whereas in England. . .'

She stopped, realising that he had pulled his chair a little closer and was watching her with a tender expression.

'In England you had a lot of worries, I believe,' he said softly. 'Your marriage wasn't easy, was it?'

She swallowed hard. 'No, it wasn't easy. I don't like to talk about it.'

He stood up and reached out his hands to pull her

into his arms. As if in a dream she allowed herself to be drawn into his sensual embrace, and she felt a deep sense of peace descending on her. This was where she belonged, with Chris. It didn't matter that he was secretive. Nothing mattered when he was so tender with her. She revelled in the feel of his lips on hers before she abandoned herself to his caresses. . .

She stirred in his arms as she felt her passion rising to match his. This was such an exquisitely dangerous situation. She was reaching the point of no return. But this was the point at which she had to come to a decision. . .did she want to give herself completely, to surrender herself to the man who had captivated her heart. . .to have an affair with a man about whom she knew so little?

It was as if Chris had sensed her change of mood and the turmoil of her emotions. Gently he eased her away from him, looking down at her with a strangely tender but incomprehensible expression.

She looked up into his eyes, wondering what thoughts were going through his head after their tender but passionate idyll. 'You're tired, aren't you?' he said gently.

Her fatigue had long since vanished, but it would be easier to say yes. She nodded, running a hand through her tousled hair.

'I think I should go to bed,' she said.

He was smiling now. 'I think you should. It will be safer. . .less complicated when you're alone in your little room. Goodnight, Sara.'

'Goodnight.' She climbed the wide wooden stairs to her room and lay down on the bed.

Her sleep when it came was fitful and full of dreams. She was walking through the clinic gardens. Chris was walking in front of her, but he didn't look round. She called his name, but he took no notice. He simply walked on.

She awoke with a feeling of helplessness. . .of not being in control of her own life. Once again she was being manipulated, used. How much of herself should she give without questioning the motives?

She showered, dressed in a clean white uniform and went down the stairs.

'So, do you feel more refreshed this morning, Sara?'

Chris was sitting out on the veranda, a glass of orange juice in his hand. The morning sun was already hot over the unsheltered rice field that bordered the trees at the edge of the garden.

'Yes, thanks,' she answered, sitting down in the bamboo chair opposite him.

He poured out some coffee and handed her a cup across the low wicker table. She helped herself to a freshly baked roll, spreading it with the fig jam.

'What's on the agenda today?' she asked. 'Should we start Nick's full treatment?'

'I don't think so,' he replied in a careful voice. 'I had a long chat with him, and he's really not ready.'

She put down her coffee-cup. 'I think you're pampering him.'

'And I think you're being impatient.'

She shrugged. 'You're the boss.'

'I am indeed.'

His tone was too hard for her liking. She'd never seen his eyes glint with such severity.

'I'd like to take Nick out today,' he continued, his tone modifying to a professional level. 'We're well staffed here, so you can come with us. Nick likes you and you understand him. . .in spite of your impatience.'

'He's very fond of Nurse Ngurah,' she said.

'So I understand. That's one complication that might be difficult to deal with if it gets out of hand.'

Sara raised her eyebrows. 'I don't see why it should. A bit of romance in the poor boy's life might solve more problems than it poses.'

Chris leaned back in his chair and observed her with a fond expression.

'Just like a woman! Love will conquer everything, won't it?'

'I'm not talking about love,' she explained. 'I'm talking about a simple innocent romance that would inject a little interest into Nick's apathetic view of life.'

'You of all people should know there's no such thing as a simple innocent romance,' he said evenly.

She felt the tension across the table as their eyes met in a long, cold appraisal.

'You're either committed or not,' he continued, in a husky voice. 'You must have been totally committed to your husband, otherwise. . .' He stopped, as if searching for the right words.

She waited for a few seconds. 'Otherwise what?' she prompted.

'Otherwise you wouldn't have stayed as long as you did.'

She remained silent, not wanting to reveal more than was necessary.

'Perhaps I wanted to stay,' she said carefully, after weighing up her words.

'I don't think so. From what you've told me I would say you were in a pretty desperate situation. And even now, three years on, you've had to leave England so that you can forget what happened. But why choose Bali?'

Sara felt the beads of sweat breaking out on her forehead. 'I was curious to see what was the attraction here,' she began carefully. 'You see. . .you see, Mike had a holiday here only weeks before he died.'

His eyes softened, taking on a sympathetic expression. 'A holiday? By himself?'

She swallowed hard as the memories flooded back. 'I don't know who was with him. I wasn't due for any leave from hospital. . . I couldn't get away when he told me he was taking a holiday. I think he might have had a girl with him. . .in fact, I'm sure he had.'

'I see. . .poor Sara!' Chris moved to her side of the table and put an arm around her shoulder.

For a brief moment she leaned her head back, feeling the comforting hard contours of his muscular chest. She hadn't meant to tell anyone of her suspicions. . . she certainly hadn't meant to tell Chris. . .but now she was glad she'd done so.

She felt his fingers gently turning her face upwards towards him. And then his lips came slowly down on to hers.

Like a flower at the end of a drought she opened her lips to savour the sweet refreshing kiss.

'I'm glad you told me, Sara,' he whispered. 'We

mustn't have secrets from each other. You can confide in me.'

'And you can confide in me,' she told him, her eyes searching his face. 'Please, Chris, tell me. . .tell me. . .'

He gave her a disarming smile as he pulled himself to his full height. 'Tell you what, Sara?'

'I think you know,' she said in a bland tone. 'The way you disappear at a moment's notice, the way nobody knows where you are, and then you reappear days later giving no explanation. Are you involved in . . .in. . .?' She couldn't bring herself to voice her fears.

'You'll have to trust me, Sara,' he told her. 'I can't tell you what I'm involved in. It would only lead to complications if I did.'

She took a deep breath, realising that she was no further on in her search for the truth. But looking up at Chris standing there on the veranda, she couldn't believe that he was involved in anything sinister. Like he said, she had to trust him.

He reached forward and pulled her to her feet. 'Go and change out of your uniform into something cool and casual. I'll go along and pick up Nick.'

'I'll need to spend half an hour with baby Deborah before we go, so I'll change after that,' Sara said quickly. 'Did you see her parents yesterday?'

Chris nodded. 'Yes, Fiona and Tim were relieved to find that their financial problems are over. I've cancelled their medical bill and told them I'll keep Deborah here for a few more weeks until she's really strong.'

'So I didn't speak out of turn?' Sara pursued, with a gentle smile on her face.

He hesitated. 'Let's say I would have preferred you not to speculate in my absence.'

She swallowed hard. He wasn't going to give in to her. 'I'll go and see to Deborah.' She turned as she left the veranda. 'Where are we going to take Nick today?'

He smiled, obviously looking forward to their expedition. 'To Goa Gajah, the mysterious elephant cave,' he told her.

As she walked across to the obstetrics unit Sara remembered that Goa Gajah was one of the places Mike had visited. He had actually had the nerve to send her a postcard from there. Yes, this was one of the Balinese tourist attractions she had hoped to see.

A couple of hours later Sara found herself staring up at the fantastically carved entrance to the elephant cave. The carvings depicted entangling leaves, animals, ocean waves, rocks, and demonic human shapes running from the gaping mouth which formed the entrance.

'What a fascinating cave!' she exclaimed, shielding her eyes from the sun. 'I suppose the huge carved earrings on that monstrous head above the entrance signify that it's supposed to be a woman. It all looks very scary.'

'Wait till you see the inside!' said Chris, taking her by the arm and moving forward.

She shivered. 'I'm not sure I want to go inside,' she told him. 'Nick, do you want to see the inside of the cave?'

'Of course,' her patient replied. He was already striding towards the fearsome hole beneath the gargantuan head.

'I'm going to stay outside in the sunshine,' she decided. 'It looks spooky in there. To be honest, I get claustrophobia in confined spaces.'

Chris laughed. 'Come on, Nick. We men will brave the interior!'

Sara watched as the two men appeared to be swallowed up by the monster's head. Nothing would induce her to follow them. Once, when she was a small child, on a school outing, she had become separated from the rest of the group at Wookey Hole Caves in Somerset. She had never forgotten the panic she'd felt at being alone, surrounded and completely enclosed by the intimidating cave walls.

But outside the sun was warm on her face. She saw that there were some excavations at the front of the cave. It looked as if it was some kind of bathing place, and she could see there were six female figures resembling nymphs or goddesses holding water spouts.

She wandered along, enjoying the sun and the freedom to do as she wished. There was a rocky slope near the cave, and she decided to climb down it and find a spot where she could soak up the sun until Chris and Nick had finished their cave exploration. She clambered over the rocks for a couple of minutes until she found the fragments of a fallen cliff face and ornamental shrine.

Deciding that this was a picturesque place to rest, she sat down on one of the boulders. There were several tourists nearby and she felt quite safe.

Take 4 Medical Romances

Mills & Boon Medical Romances capture all the excitement and emotion of a busy medical world... A world, however, where love and romance are never far away.

We will send you **4 MEDICAL ROMANCES** absolutely **FREE** plus a cuddly teddy bear and a mystery gift, as your introduction to this superb series.

At the same time we'll reserve a subscription for you to our Reader Service.

Every month you could receive the 4 latest Medical Romances delivered direct to your door postage and packing **FREE**, plus a free Newsletter filled with competitions, author news and much more.

And remember there's no obligation, you may cancel or suspend your subscription at any time. So you've nothing to lose and a world of romance to gain!

Your Free Gifts! Return this card, and we'll send you a lovely little soft brown bear together with a mystery gift... So don't delay!

FILL IN THE FREE BOOKS COUPON OVERLEAF

NO STAMP NEEDED

FREE BOOKS COUPON

YES Please send me 4 FREE Medical Romances together with my teddy bear and mystery gift. Please also reserve a special Reader Service subscription for me. If I decide to subscribe, I will receive 4 brand new books for just £6.40 each month, postage and packing free. If, however, I decide not to subscribe, I shall write to you within 10 days. The free books and gifts will be mine to keep in anycase. I understand that I am under no obligation - I may cancel or suspend my subscription at any time simply by writing to you. I am over 18 years of age.

EXTRA BONUS

We all love mysteries, so as well as the FREE books and Teddy, here's an intriguing gift especially for you. No clues - send off today!

12A2D

Ms/Mrs/Miss/Mr _____

Address _____

_____

Postcode _____ Signature _____

One per household. Offer expires 31st January 1993. The right is reserved to refuse an application and change the terms of this offer. Readers in Southern Africa write to Book Services International Ltd. P.O. Box 41654, Craighall, Transvaal 2024. Other Overseas and Eire, send for details. You may be mailed with other offers from other reputable companies as a result of this application. If

Reader Service
FREEPOST
P.O. Box 236
Croydon
CR9 9EL

SEND NO MONEY NOW

Suddenly a hand touched her arm, and she tensed. A young man was staring into her face.

'The doctor. . .where is he?' he asked anxiously.

The young man had a strange accent—possibly French, possibly Spanish, she couldn't tell. His face was dark, weatherbeaten, and he had the appearance of someone who was sleeping rough. His clothes were dirty, dishevelled, torn. But it was his hollow eyes that alarmed her.

'Do you mean Dr Stephens?' she asked warily.

The young man was still holding on to her arm. She attempted to shake him off, but his broken nails dug into her skin.

'I must see him! Where is he?'

'I left him up there in the cave, but. . .'

The young man released his grip and started to clamber up the rocky hillside. Sara watched him go, rubbing her arm to ease the discomfort. What a wild-looking youth! she thought as she watched his progress up the hillside. She hoped Chris would be able to handle him.

She stood up and started back up the hill. She was out of breath when she reached the flat ground in front of the cave. Nick and Chris were just emerging, and she tensed as she saw the strange young man standing behind the carved stone at the side of the cave, hidden from sight. He waited until Nick had walked away before emerging to confront Chris.

But, contrary to what she had expected, Chris showed no surprise. He appeared to listen to the young man for a few seconds before holding out his hand to take something.

Sara held her breath. The young man had moved away into the crowd of tourists. Nick was looking around, wondering where Dr Stephens had got to. He saw Sara and smiled.

'There you are! For a moment I thought you'd both abandoned me.'

Chris came striding over to join them, a bland smile on his handsome face.

'What a fantastic cave!' exclaimed Nick. 'Pity you missed it, Sister.'

'Oh, there was plenty to see out here,' Sara told him. She turned to look at Chris. 'What did that young man want?'

Chris's eyes gave nothing away as he looked down at her. 'What young man?'

CHAPTER NINE

THIS was the day they were to start the full treatment with Nick. That was the first waking thought that came to Sara as she stretched out on her comfortable bed, basking in the early morning sunshine, listening to the cries of the varied birds and animals in the garden.

It wasn't going to be easy.

But her second thought disturbed her even more. Chris's continued refusal to confide in her.

It was two whole weeks since their trip to Goa Gajah, the elephant cave, but Chris had studiously avoided her questions about the strange young man who had confronted him. Sara was even beginning to doubt herself whether he existed. Had she dreamed up the whole incident? Had she fallen asleep in the hot sunshine and experienced some sort of illusion? The tropical sun could do wickedly disturbing things to the brain.

She climbed out of bed and searched her face in the mirror for signs of strain. No, she was perfectly normal, perfectly in control of her faculties, and it was Chris who was pulling the wool over her eyes. But meanwhile she had her patients to take care of. She hadn't time to worry about her distracting relationship with Chris.

She showered and dressed in full uniform. This was one day when she wanted to be totally professional. Nick was going to need all the help she could give him.

She had a hasty breakfast alone on the veranda. Chris, it appeared, had already gone on duty.

She found him with Nick; he was sitting beside his patient deep in conversation when she arrived.

Chris looked up as she went in and smiled. 'I thought I'd make an early start today. I'll need to go away for a couple of days.'

She felt her spirits drop. 'But we agreed to carry out Nick's treatment together!'

'Nick's going to be fine,' Chris assured her. 'We've just had a long talk about what's going to happen. I actually took him off all drugs last night, and look at him!'

Nick stood up and gave Sara a beaming smile as if to demonstrate his good health.

'I'm just off to the swimming pool, so I'll see you people later,' he said jauntily, slinging a towel over his shoulder and grabbing a pair of swimming trunks.

Sara waited until he had gone. 'Nick's obviously going to be all right for the first few hours, but what happens then? Supposing I can't handle him while you're away? The second and third day of withdrawal symptoms can be agony for some patients.'

Chris moved towards her and put his hands on her shoulders, looking down at her with sympathetic eyes.

'I know it's going to be tough, but I have absolute faith in you, Sara. I know you can cope—you've had experience of patients like this. And if you need help, Dr Astuti will be close at hand.'

'I want a male nurse on hand twenty-four hours a day,' she said firmly.

Chris nodded. 'That goes without saying. I've

already sent a message to Sister Poleng asking her to assign someone as from this morning.'

Sara breathed a sigh of relief. 'Well, it looks as if you're not indispensable after all, so there's nothing to keep you here. I'll expect you back when I see you.'

She turned and started to move away, but Chris caught her by the arm.

'I wouldn't go if I didn't have to,' he said quietly.

She looked up into his eyes, feeling again the surge of excitement that flooded through her whenever she was near him.

'I'm going to miss you, Sara,' he added.

She stood absolutely still, her heart pounding, knowing that he was going to kiss her and that she felt powerless to resist.

'One day you must take me with you on one of your assignments,' she said. 'One day. . .'

But his lips silenced her in a long, tender kiss.

'One day I will take you with me,' he said as he pulled himself away.

She searched his face for signs of sincerity, for something that would show he wasn't just fobbing her off again.

'Promise?' she whispered.

'I promise,' he told her solemnly. 'Trust me, Sara.'

She gave him a gentle smile. If only she could!

She cared for Nick for the next two days with the help of a rota of male nurses. When she took some off-duty time she assigned Nurse Vanessa Williams to take her place. And at night, the night sister kept a special watch on Nick.

But on the third morning Sara was awakened by a thunderous knocking on her door.

'Sister, come quickly! You're wanted in the medical unit.'

She recognised the houseboy's voice as she drifted out from her deep sleep. Her mind switched on immediately. It had to be a problem with Nick.

Hurriedly she threw on the uniform dress she had worn the previous evening and got herself outside into the clinic garden. The sun was low in the sky, setting orange flames over the smaller bushes at the edge of the garden.

She could hear shouting as she hurried along the corridor of the medical unit. Nick's door was wide open. A couple of male nurses were holding him down, and the night sister was remonstrating with him.

'Dr Stephens said no medication under any circumstances!' the night sister was shouting. 'You have to understand it's all for your own good.'

'Thank you, Sister, I'll take over,' Sara said quietly, appalled at her patient's distressed condition.

Nick's eyes were streaming and he was shaking violently. He barely seemed to recognise her when she approached his bed and sat down on the edge.

'I wouldn't sit there if I were you,' said one of the male nurses. 'He got violent with me a few minutes ago. That's when I sent for you.'

'Do something for me!' Nick wailed plaintively, trying to reach out to Sara. His eyes focused on her and he realised at last who she was.

Sara looked up at the night sister. 'You can leave Nick to me,' she said. 'He won't harm me.'

'Well, if you're sure. . .'

'I'm sure,' she said, with a confidence she didn't feel. She knew she had to defuse the situation, and the belligerent attitude of the other staff wasn't helping.

'I'll leave the door open,' the night sister told her. 'I'm just down the corridor if you need me, and Dr Astuti will be along presently.'

'Thank you, Sister.' Sara couldn't wait to be alone with her patient.

She put out her hand and placed it over Nick's clammy skin. 'I'll stay with you, Nick,' she told him gently. 'I know what you're going through.'

'No, you don't! Nobody does. I can't take it. . .I can't!'

She heard steps in the corridor and found herself wondering if Dr Astuti would be as unsympathetic as the others. She would have to stay here until. . .

'Chris!' She felt the relief flooding through her. 'You came back early!'

'What's happening here?' He strode into the room. 'Where are the male nurses?'

'They're having a rest.' Sara tried to indicate from her tone that she didn't want to discuss the situation in front of the patient.

'Poor Nick!' Chris sat down at the other side of the bed.

The young patient reached out his arms like a child and held on to the doctor. 'Help me, Doctor,' he begged.

'I'll help you, Nick. Sister Freeman and I will stay with you until you're well. One or the other of us will be here all the time.'

Sara's eyes met Chris's over the head of the patient and she silently nodded her agreement. She was rewarded by the look of appreciation in Chris's eyes. It was going to be tough for all of them.

It was two weeks since Nick's cold turkey treatment had started. .Sara realised they weren't yet out of the wood, but when she went in to check on her patient he was actually smiling. What a relief!

As she placed the thermometer under Nick's tongue she remembered what a strain the last couple of weeks had been for Chris and herself. For eight days they had alternated a continual vigil between them. They had eased off for the last couple of days, but had always remained on call in the clinic compound.

'Normal temperature again, Nick,' she told him. 'I'm going to let you go for a swim tomorrow.'

'Really? Thanks, Sister. You've been great! I couldn't have done it without you and Dr Stephens.'

Sara knew that was certainly true. She went out into the corridor, feeling a real sense of achievement. There had been times during those early days when she had wondered what on earth had made her join the medical profession. And Chris had actually admitted feeling the same sentiments during one long, difficult day when Nick was suffering badly.

But now, as she swung along the corridor out into the late afternoon sun, she remembered how the experience had brought her so much closer to Chris. Together they had held on, encouraging their patient when they both felt utterly exhausted, badgering, cajoling, exhorting. . .

Chris was standing in the middle of the path, waiting for her to catch up with him.

'How's Nick?' he asked.

'Fine! I think we've won.'

He smiled. 'So do I. So I think it's about time I let you out of this prison. How about that meal I promised you a couple of weeks ago? You were too tired, I remember. You're probably exhausted now, but as your personal physician I would recommend a night on the town.'

'Oh, Chris!' Sara drew in her breath before she said too much. She didn't want him to know how much she had regretted not taking up his offer on that first night here at the Temple Clinic. She had thought she was going to be so clever with her wiles, trapping him into confiding in her. But it hadn't worked, nor did she care any more. She had come to love him so much during the time they'd worked together with their drug patient. She had come to admire his strength of character, his calm soothing bedside manner, the way he always knew exactly how to handle a difficult patient. . .

'Yes?' he queried. 'You're taking a long time to give me an answer. I'm only asking you out for the evening—it's not going to be the Royal Garden Party! What's the problem?'

She smiled. 'No problem, Chris. I'd love to go out this evening.'

He smiled back. 'Good. I'll book the table. Now come along and have a look at baby Deborah with me. The nurse you assigned to her while you worked with Nick has been very conscientious, but I think the parents will want you with me when I give them a full report this afternoon. They seem to regard you as Deborah's surrogate mum because you brought her into the world, so to speak.'

'Deborah's very special to me. I've been keeping tabs on her even when I worked with Nick. I always spent a few minutes with her when I could spare the time. Her fingernails are starting to grow and she's got a fine dusting of blonde hair. . .oh, she's gorgeous!'

Sara broke off, slightly embarrassed at her own enthusiasm.

Chris's eyes held a tender expression. 'You love babies, don't you?'

She nodded. 'I'm going to miss Deborah when she goes.'

'Don't worry,' he said, in a husky voice, 'that won't be for some time. I never allow a prem out until I'm confident about the lungs.'

'But can the parents afford to stay on?' queried Sara.

'Tim works as a clerk in a travel agents back home, and they've promised to keep his job until he gets back. He's an enterprising young man. He's got himself a job in one of the restaurants as a waiter. It doesn't pay very much, but it's enough for the small bill they have to pay at the *losmen*. And I could always help them out if they got in a fix.'

'I'm sure you could.' Sara began walking quickly over in the direction of the obstetrics unit. 'Let's go and take a look at Deborah.'

The sun was setting behind the trees that bordered the west veranda as Sara and Chris sipped their drinks. Sara had a deep sense of satisfaction.

'It's been a good day,' she said happily. 'Nick over the worst and Deborah beginning to look like a normal full-term baby.'

Chris smiled, stretching out his hand to grasp hers across the table.

'This is why we keep on when the going gets tough—because we know it will be worth it in the end. Remember that night when we both had to stay with Nick? When he was threatening to kill himself if either of us left the room?'

She shivered. 'Don't I just! I don't know what I would have done without you, Chris.'

'The feeling's mutual, Sara,' he said huskily. 'We make a good team.'

'When we're both pulling together,' she said evenly.

She felt his fingers relax; he took his hand away and stood up decisively as if he feared she might start to question him again.

The Tjampuhan Hotel was over the Campuan Bridge, set on the side of a magnificent gorge. They parked the car out at the front and walked inside to find a large, airy, spacious dining-room open at one end to give a magnificent view of the ravine.

From their table they could see the green slope of the other side of the ravine lit up by iridescent lights discreetly hidden among the tall tropical trees.

'It looks like fairyland over there. . .it's all so beautiful!' smiled Sara.

All around her was the ornately carved interior and in front of her she could see where the garden sloped away on various levels, each one illuminated to display the exotic plants surrounding a tiny stream that formed pools for the fish and the frogs.

Chris smiled. 'I'm glad you approve. I meant to bring you here on your first night in Ubud. . .but better late than never.'

'A lot has happened since that first night,' she said, half to herself.

'But we understand one another better than we did,' he added softly.

She watched his face in the candlelit glow. The magic had returned. She was in love with Chris. If only she knew how he felt. . .oh, she knew he could be roused passionately, but was it simply physical desire, or did he have this deep down longing she felt? If only she could strip away that superficial, self-confident, devil-may-care veneer!

They had fresh asparagus, followed by delicious Balinese smoked duckling. Afterwards they took their coffee to a little table halfway down the garden and sat, beneath pretty Chinese lanterns, listening to the croaking of the frogs and the rushing of the stream as it rippled over the rocks to join the river in the valley.

'I have to go away tomorrow,' Chris said suddenly.

Sara drew in her breath. She wasn't going to spoil this wonderful evening. The time they'd spent together had been very precious. And she knew that no amount of questioning would elicit information from Chris. She wouldn't even ask him how long he was going to be away.

She put down her coffee-cup. 'I think we should leave now,' she said.

He put out his hand. 'Not yet, Sara. . . Would you like to go with me tomorrow?'

Her eyes widened in disbelief. 'Why. . .? I mean. . .' She stopped in mid-sentence, unwilling to voice her thoughts.

'I feel I owe you some sort of explanation. You've been very patient with me. . .too patient, perhaps. But I had to be sure.'

She was totally at a loss. 'Sure of what?'

'Sure that I could trust you,' he explained.

'Trust me?' Her voice rose as she felt the anger and frustration that had been eating inside her rise to the surface. 'That's rich, coming from you! You're the one who goes swanning off at a moment's notice. You're the one who won't discuss where you're going. I have to stay behind, not knowing where you are, what you're up to. . .' She stopped and took a deep breath to calm herself. 'For all I know you could be involved in. . . in. . .'

Chris's eyes gleamed. 'Say it, Sara. Put it into words.'

She closed her eyes in a vain attempt to blot out the horror of her suspicions. 'I can't! I've been through all that before, and now. . .'

She felt his arms around her and opened her eyes.

'You're safe with me, Sara. I won't betray you. . .as Mike did.'

'But I haven't told you anything about Mike. . .' she began.

'You don't have to,' he told her in a husky voice. 'I already know. In fact, I probably know more about Mike than you do.'

She stirred in his arms, pulling herself away so that

she could look up into those deep dark mysterious eyes.

'What are you saying? How can you know about Mike? You'd never heard of him until I. . .' She stopped, feeling the suspicious pounding of her heart. 'Did you know who I was when I arrived in Bali?' she demanded.

Chris tried to pull her back into his arms, but she resisted him.

'Yes, I knew,' he told her gently. 'What I didn't know was that Mike had operated completely on his own. . .that you had absolutely no idea what he was up to when he was here three years ago.'

An awful fear was clawing at the back of her mind. 'But when I came here you thought it might be to revive Mike's activities on the drugs scene. . .is that it?'

He ran a hand through his unruly brown hair. 'I didn't know you at all,' he said carefully. 'But a number of people who are working to eradicate the drugs scene out here had their suspicions about you. . . That's why I couldn't confide in you. But in the last couple of weeks I've come to know you so well that I can't hold out on you any longer.'

'Did you actually meet Mike when he was out here?' she asked.

He shook his head. 'He was only here for a short time. But the authorities were on to him. They knew he was trying to arrange a shipment of drugs over to England.'

'That must have been the cargo that arrived the night Mike died,' Sara said, as if in a dream. 'He'd been away for several weeks. I'd gone back to the house for a weekend off duty. I remember it was almost midnight when I heard the helicopters overhead, and I looked out through the bedroom window. A police car was pulling in to the drive...'

She stopped, unable to continue until she'd caught her breath again.

'The police were very kind to me when they broke the news that Mike had crashed his car down near the waterfront. Apparently he'd been trying to avoid them all the way back from London. They said they had reason to suspect that he was involved with the consignment of drugs they'd just apprehended from a newly arrived ship in the estuary. They questioned me and searched the house, but Mike hadn't left any clues, and it was obvious that he hadn't confided in me...at least, I thought it was... I've sometimes wondered if I've been under surveillance.'

'I think the matter was tied up satisfactorily in England,' Chris told her. 'No one has ever doubted you there, but out here it's a different matter.'

'Why?' she asked.

He paused, weighing up his words carefully. 'I don't want to frighten you, but there are people who disapproved of Mike trying to muscle in on the act...people who would be disturbed to know that you're Mike's widow. That's why I'm glad you kept your maiden name. Tomorrow, when I take you to Lake Batur, you mustn't tell anyone who you are. The patients we care for up there may have heard of Mike.'

Sara frowned. 'What kind of a medical situation are

you dealing with at Lake Batur?' she asked, feeling a wave of apprehension.

He took a deep breath. 'I'm trying to establish a rehabilitation from drug dependency clinic near the shores of Lake Batur. That's where a number of young drug addicts set up camp some time ago. There are a lot of young people who drop out these days and simply wander around the Far East, where it's cheaper to live. But if they get into the clutches of the drug pushers they're on a downward path. I've received a lot of opposition to the clinic I'm setting up out there from the local inhabitants, and also from the Balinese authorities. No one wants drug addicts living near them. I'm having to tread very carefully. At the moment my clinic is, in effect, illegal, but I'm going to keep on fighting. I can't let these young people down.'

Sara moved back towards him, feeling once again the admiration for him as a dedicated doctor. But it was disturbing to think that he was only now beginning to trust her. She cast her mind fleetingly back to those early days of her relationship with him. Had he deliberately led her on so that he could worm his way into her confidence? Maybe he had, but she wasn't going to dwell on it. He trusted her now...just as she trusted him.

'We'd better go back,' he told her. 'Tomorrow is going to be a long hard day.'

'What about Nick?' she asked. 'Won't he miss us if we're both away?'

'We're taking Nick with us,' he told her. 'He's ready for some group therapy, and my clinic at Lake Batur is the only place he'll get it.'

'What about Deborah?' she asked. 'I hate to be separated from her. How long will we be away?'

'A few days at the most,' he assured her. 'Deborah will be well cared for. I'm pleased with her progress.'

He took her hand as they climbed back up the path to the dining-room. Most of the diners had left. Sara looked across at the table where they'd enjoyed their dinner. A sudden breeze from the garden disturbed the flowers in the vase; the candle spluttered and died.

She looked away, focusing her eyes on Chris as he escorted her to the door. The old era of distrust was over. . .the new was just beginning. But had she finally exorcised the ghosts of the past?

The moon was shining full on the veranda as they said goodnight. When they kissed, Sara felt as if the world was standing still. So much of the puzzle surrounding Chris had been resolved tonight, but she couldn't help wondering if he was still holding out on her. He had proved himself to be such a master of subterfuge. Even as his enticing lips claimed hers she prayed that this display of tenderness wasn't a ploy to hold her confidence.

He'd said he trusted her. . .what were his words worth?

But as the deep, sensuous desire within her rose to the surface she abandoned her fears. The romantic feelings coursing through her veins were lifting her on to a higher plane, blotting out all unwelcome thoughts.

She was sure of only one thing. She loved Chris. . . and he loved her. . .didn't he?

CHAPTER TEN

THEY were driving north along a twisty, twiny, dusty road between lush green paddy fields where the workers sweltered in the already hot mid-morning sun. Chris tightened his grip on the steering-wheel as they climbed higher into the hills, negotiating difficult and dangerous bends in the rock-strewn road.

Children played beside the roadside in one village as they bathed in the stream that trickled along through the main street. They waved to the Land Rover, their bright smiles lighting up the attractive dark features. Sara waved back.

'I'm going to miss Deborah,' she said to Chris.

He took his eyes off the road for an instant and smiled at her.

'You won't have time to think about her—the work up in the hills is totally absorbing. It's going to take all your skills as a nursing sister.'

Sara turned to look at Nick, hunched up in the back seat, sound asleep.

'Was Nick pleased to be transferred?' she whispered.

'He wanted to take Nurse Ngurah with us,' Chris told her. 'But that would be out of the question. You're the only person from the Temple Clinic to be introduced to the situation at Batur. The fewer people know about it, the better. . .that is, until it's officially recognised.'

'You're very sure of yourself,' she remarked. 'What if you're unsuccessful?'

'I never accept defeat,' he assured her.

'I haven't told you this before,' she began carefully. 'but one of the things that worried me about you when I first met you was your over-confidence. Mike was like that. He wouldn't accept defeat. I used to think he lived in cloud cuckoo land.'

'Maybe he did...but I don't. Mike was working on the wrong side of the law and couldn't possibly succeed in his ill-chosen ventures.'

Sara remained quiet, not wanting to break up the new rapport that existed between them. She could have pointed out that Chris, in his characteristically devil-may-care attitude, was running an illegal clinic. Surely that constituted being on the wrong side of the law, didn't it? She only hoped he hadn't bitten off more than he could chew.

They were climbing up through a forest of bamboo. As they emerged from the trees Sara caught her breath at the sheer magnificence of the landscape. Spread out below the road was a huge volcanic basin. Black ribbons of lava ran down from the misty peak beyond the valley.

Chris pulled the car to the side of the road and pointed to the mysterious, obscured mountain summit.

'There it is... Mount Batur. The Balinese have a legend which tells how the sacred Hindu mountain Mahameru was divided into two and placed in Bali as the volcanoes Agung and Batur. Next to Agung—which is over there in the mist—Batur is the most revered mountain in Bali. There's supposed to be a god living on its summit, and there are temples all over the island where this god is worshipped.'

He broke off with a wry grin. 'You can see the sort of opposition I'm meeting in challenging the status quo out here! I'm having to tread very carefully. On the one hand I don't want to spoil the legendary, sacred atmosphere of the area, but on the other I have to save the lives of my unfortunate patients.'

He started up the Land Rover again and began to negotiate a difficult descent of hairpin bends to the floor of the volcanic valley. They stopped beside the lake and he pointed out some natural hot springs.

'Nature's sauna,' he said. 'Many a weary traveller stops here for a refreshing dip in the waters. This is where some of my patients arrive. They've been told about my clinic by word of mouth, and they know it's somewhere near here. I usually try to arrange for someone to watch out for them. Stay here with Nick while I go and check it out for myself.'

The hot springs appeared to be deserted. After making a brief inspection Chris drove off again along the road that skirted the lake.

On either side of them, Sara could see wild, rugged boulders of black lava. It was a desolate scene; it reminded her of the pictures she'd seen of the surface of the moon.

A thin drizzle had begun and a mist was descending on the lake. Sara shivered. She actually felt cold for the first time since arriving in Bali. It was a novel experience.

Within seconds the drizzle had turned into a full-scale downpour. Chris wound up the windows and set the windscreen wipers on full.

'It's bleak out here,' Sara remarked, feeling the chill affecting her spirits. She was wishing she were back in the predictable warmth of the Temple Clinic. 'Is the volcano still active?'

'Who knows?' shrugged Chris as he turned off the narrow lakeside road. 'It erupted in 1917, destroying many homes, temples and more than a thousand lives. The village of Batur was swallowed up by lava which stopped short of the foot of the temple. The villagers thought this must be a good omen, and stayed on. But in 1926 another eruption buried the entire temple except for the highest shrine, and the villagers were forced to move to the top of the high cliffs up there behind us. But they took their salvaged shrine with them and built a new temple.'

'I can see why the people should have a great reverence for this area,' Sara said quietly. 'They've been through so much that they've built up a resistance to any form of change.'

'Exactly!' said Chris. 'Now you're beginning to see the problem I'm up against. But can't you just feel the intriguing atmosphere of the place. . .the scope and possibilities it offers us?'

As they bumped along the unmade boulder-strewn track deluged by the rain, Sara found it hard to share his enthusiasm.

'Quite frankly, the place give me the creeps!' she said, shivering with cold and trying to move her cramped limbs.

Chris laughed, reaching across to catch hold of her hand.

'We're nearly there. You can have a hot drink to revive you.'

The contrast between the stark simplicity of the drug dependency clinic and the overt luxury of Chris's other clinics was immediately obvious.

'Is this it?' Sara asked in disbelief as Chris stopped the Land Rover in front of a large wooden cabin reminiscent of the something out of a Wild West movie.

'Not much to look at, but it's the work that goes on inside that's important,' he explained, jumping down and sprinting around to open Sara's door.

He held out his arms and helped her down to the wet, muddy track. For a moment their bodies touched and Sara forgot the pouring rain. She could almost feel the beating of Chris's heart against her own. She held her breath until he relaxed his sensuous grip.

'Run along inside before you get drenched!' he said, releasing her. 'Nick, wake up! We're here.'

The interior of the cabin felt warm and cosy as she hurried in through the front door. A young man with blond tousled curly hair, wearing a yellow T-shirt and faded blue jeans, greeted her with an outstretched hand.

'Hi—I'm Dr Frank Green. You must be Sister Freeman. I've heard a lot about you from Chris. I'm glad he finally decided to bring you out here. We could do with another pair of hands.'

'I don't know how long I'm staying,' Sara said quickly, her eyes roving around the rustic room. Apart from folding chairs stacked against the wall and a long trestle table there was no other furniture.

Chris arrived with Nick, stumbling in and slamming the door against the inclement weather.

'You're just in time for lunch,' Dr Green said. 'Grab yourselves a chair.'

Several young men began to drift into the room, and Sara saw that the accent was on ultra-casual clothes. Many of the garments were patched and darned, but they were mostly clean, although crumpled. All the young men appeared to know the drill. They each took a chair and pulled it up to the scrubbed trestle-table.

One of the men was carrying a huge soup cauldron which he placed on the table. A couple of men followed on with bowls, spoons and a basket of bread cut into huge chunks.

The soup was spicy and hot; some kind of vegetable to which root ginger had been added, Sara decided, as she took her first tentative sip.

Chris was watching her from across the other side of the table, and he smiled.

'We have some good cooks here. Everybody has to try their hand while they're here, we're a totally independent community. You'd be surprised at the number of skills that emerge. Take Frank, for example. I didn't know he was a doctor when he first came here.'

Dr Green gave a wry grin. 'I'd been bumming around the Far East since qualifying. I didn't know what I wanted to do. I got hooked on drugs and didn't know how to get off them till I met Chris. I've been cured for twelve months now. . .when I say cured, I mean I live one day at a time. I haven't taken drugs for twelve months and I don't ever intend to again.'

Sara studied the faces of the men sitting around the table as she heard Chris beginning to explain the situation.

'Everyone who comes here has had a problem with drugs. We detoxify them and provide rehabilitation through self-help groups. The patients pool their resources to keep the place going, and I only step in to help if there's an emergency.'

He looked across the table and gave Sara a wry grin. 'When there's an emergency I may be called here at a moment's notice.'

Sara smiled as their eyes met. 'Point taken,' she said quietly.

The men around the table were talking vociferously, oblivious to Sara and Chris. They had already been accepted into the community as worthwhile, trusted members of staff. Sara felt a sudden pang of fear as she remembered Chris's warning that she must keep her identity secret. She cast a sideways glance at the man next to her. He was older than the rest. She wondered how long he had been out here in Bali. Had he been there three years ago when Mike had made his unpopular attempt to get in on the drugs scene?

Don't think about it! she told herself as she finished up her soup. So long as they all knew her as Sister Freeman she would come to no harm.

There was papaya and mangoes to follow, after which everyone helped with the general clearing away. The bowls were taken outside the back door which led off from the room that served as a kitchen.

Sara was glad the rain had stopped as she stood in line to wash her bowl under a cold water tap. Behind the cabin she could see the sun shining on the slope of the hill that led to the rim of the volcanic crater. The grass was sparse and shrivelled. The whole area appeared desolate and inhospitable. But it was an ideal hideaway for a clinic that no one wanted. . .no one, that was, except the patients.

Chris took her into a room beside the kitchen where there were three bedridden patients, pitiful young men who pulled their sheets up to their chins and looked at Sara with suspicion.

'We're trying to do what we can here,' Chris explained, taking Sara on one side. 'It may be weeks before these patients are strong enough to start the rehabilitation treatment. They were very weak when they came to us. I'd like you to work with them while you're here. Basically it's general nursing care and administration of the relevant medication. I've written everything on their charts. We can't wean them off drugs until their general condition has improved.'

Sara nodded. 'Haven't you got any nursing staff here?' she queried.

Chris shook his head. 'I have to rely on the patients who are well enough to help. Frank does his best to help and supervise them, but it would be good to have another member of staff here. I come here periodically if there's a medical problem they can't handle. I'll take you round and introduce you to these patients. They're understandably suspicious at first, but you'll soon gain their confidence,' he finished.

Sara took a deep breath. 'I'll do my best,' she promised.

She spent the afternoon sorting out the needs of the bed patients. With the help of one of the ambulant patients who had been a male nurse, she gave them all a bed-bath, and clean sheets.

Another patient came into the room as she was piling up the dirty sheets and whisked them away to wash them in the stream behind the cabin.

'Wouldn't it be a good idea to invest in a washing machine?' she asked Chris when he came back at the end of his afternoon spent giving all the patients a thorough examination and listening to their problems.

He smiled, indulgently. 'It would if we had any electricity, but we've only got oil lamps. Talking of which, I'll go and help with the lighting up.'

Sara glanced out of the window. The sun was low in the sky and there was a cold eerie light outside, reminding her that it was almost twilight. She wondered how long it would be before she felt at home in this unusual clinic.

Chris returned with a lantern in his hand and suggested that they have a cold beer on the veranda, soaking up the last rays of the sun.

They carried a couple of foldaway chairs outside, and Sara sank down on to one of them, sipping her beer from the can.

'When in Rome,' she said, with a wry grin.

Chris laughed. 'I'm glad you're adapting to our rough-and-ready ways. This is one reason why I'd hesistate to bring any of the nursing staff out here. They may not be as adaptable as you are.'

She leaned back against the uncomfortable chair. 'I'll take that as a compliment.'

She looked out across the lunar-type landscape that sloped down to the lake.

'It doesn't look quite so unfriendly as it did when we arrived,' she said. 'I might be able to survive a couple of days here.'

Chris smiled, his eyes tender as he looked down at her. 'I hope so, because I need your help here. You're going to be invaluable.'

She met his gaze. 'If I didn't know you better, Chris Stephens, I'd say you're piling on the compliments with an ulterior motive! You're going to ask me to stay on indefinitely.'

He laughed. 'I wouldn't be so unfeeling. . .at least I'd give you a couple of hours' warning.'

She pretended to aim a blow to his head. He caught her hand and pulled her against him, the rough wooden chairs creaking in protest.

His kiss was tender, and she responded in the same vein, revelling in their new-found closeness.

As she pulled herself away she looked up into his dark unfathomable eyes and saw a deep, enigmatic expression.

'You know, I wish I could understand you, Chris,' she told him. 'It doesn't make sense that a man of your obvious talents and qualifications would want to turn down a prestigious surgical post in London to bury himself in the middle of nowhere.'

She felt him tense. For a long time he was silent, and she began to wish she'd kept quiet.

'Look, I'm sorry I said that. I meant it as a compliment. I wasn't asking for an explanation, I was simply. . .'

'Nevertheless, you're going to get one,' he broke in urgently. 'It's about time you understood the situation.'

She saw the drained expression on his handsome features and felt a chill running through her.

'As I told you when you first came out, I was keen on surgery. . . I got the surgery prize for my year. My future at St Teresa's looked extremely rosy. I went home to tell my wife. . .'

'Your wife?' she broke in, unable to conceal her surprise.

He gave a tired smile. 'You're not the only one who's been married. I was married when I was twenty-one, to another medical student. Clare was very beautiful, very talented, and very happy to drop out of med. school when she started having our baby. She insisted she wanted to interrupt her career until our family was grown up.'

Sara held her breath. She could tell from the dark tone of Chris's voice that there was some impending tragedy.

'Our baby was a girl. . .Samantha,' he said huskily. 'But she was born several weeks prematurely. Her lungs were immature.'

'On, no!' Sara whispered under her breath, as she saw the look of despair on his face.

'As soon as she was five pounds in weight we took her home. Clare was a perfect mum. She looked after her night and day while I was studying hard for my finals. . .but one morning when we woke up. . .it was when Samantha was three months old. . .we found her lying still and quiet in her cot. She'd stopped breathing. I gave her the kiss of life; I tried everything to resuscitate her, but it was no good.'

Sara felt Chris's fingers tightening over her own. She longed to say a word of comfort, but knew there was nothing that would help. Chris had obviously come to terms with the situation. It was only when unsuspecting people like herself dragged the subject back into his consciousness that he suffered again. But now that she had got him to talk it was better if he got everything off his chest.

'And your wife?' she prompted gently. 'How did she take it?'

He ran a hand through his hair with a distracted motion. 'Very badly. On the surface she seemed very calm. It was only later that I found out that she'd started taking drugs to calm herself and help her to forget.'

He paused, and Sara could hear his rasping breathing as he searched for the right words.

'And so, on the day that I was offered a plum job in surgery, I went home to find my wife had taken an overdose from which she didn't recover. No one knows whether it was intentional or whether she just lost count of how much she was taking—that's the awful thing about dependency on drugs. But that was when I decided to leave England so that I could do something about the problem. Because if we could eradicate the people who make a vast living from drugs we would be halfway to solving the problem.'

Neither of them spoke for a few minutes. Sara looked out towards the lake. The sun had sunk beneath the hillside leaving the volcanic crater in a wilderness of darkness. Beside her a large coloured moth fluttered near the flame of the oil lamp.

At last she found her voice. 'I'm sorry, Chris,' she said softly. 'I had no idea. You always seemed so. . .'

'So happy, so carefree,' he supplied in a bright, artificial tone. 'That's the image I've portrayed ever since I came out here, and it's stuck with me. But that's not the real me.'

'I know that. . .now,' she said gently. 'I'm glad you told me about. . .about the sadness in your life. I understand you so much better.'

He held out his hand. 'We'd better go in and help to organise the supper. I don't know who's cooking this evening, but something smells good.'

She smiled. 'Thanks for taking me into your confidence, Chris. Please don't hold out on me again.'

For a moment his eyes flickered in the lamplight and she felt a moment of disquiet.

'There are some things that are better kept secret.' he said gently. 'But I don't want you to worry yourself. Just do your job. . .and trust me.'

He bent his head and kissed her tenderly on the lips.

CHAPTER ELEVEN

IT WAS such a relief to get back to the Temple Clinic! Sara found her spirits lifting as soon as Chris drove them in through the gates.

'You're glad to be back, aren't you?' he remarked, with a wry grin.

She smiled, as he helped her down from the Land Rover. 'Let's say I'm relieved to have survived. And I'm looking forward to getting back to the comfort of my own little apartment. Do you mind if I take some free time before I go on duty?'

'Have the day off, by all means. Get yourself sorted out. I'm going to go and check with Dr Astuti, but there's no need for you to come with me.'

'Thanks.' She knew she was going to need a whole day to recover from her ordeal.

As she went down through the clinic garden towards the house she revelled in her new-found freedom. It had been claustrophobic at the Batur clinic, and she'd felt so much frustration at the problems they were facing. Until Chris could get the clinic on an official footing they would make slow progress.

She had felt apprehensive at leaving Nick behind, but Chris had assured her that it was the best thing for him. Their patient needed the companionship of other patients who had been through the same detoxification programme. He required group therapy and would benefit from Dr Frank Green's considerable professional and personal experience.

Sara reached the house at the edge of the garden ravine and stepped on to the tiled veranda. Kicking off her sandals, she left them ouside beside the ornamental stone elephants as she walked barefoot into the house and over the polished floor.

The fan in the roof was cool and soothing to her hot skin. Home at last! she thought happily as she climbed up the wide wooden staircase.

She reflected that she had only been away for three days, but it felt like a lifetime! The poky little room she had been allocated in the Batur cabin had been about about the size of a broom cupboard. In fact, in the middle of one of her sleepless nights, as she'd tossed and turned on the hard camp-bed, she had decided it must actually have been a broom cupboard, hastily converted to accommodate her by one of the well-meaning patients.

Chris had been given a camp-bed in the main dormitory with the other men. She had been able to hear the varied snores drifting through the thin partition and had decided to count her blessings and not complain. If she had had any notion of a romantic couple of days with Chris, the bleak situation at Batur had put a dampener on her ideas.

The door to her sitting-room was wide open. Ahmed, the houseboy, was just leaving after his morning clean. She could see fresh flowers on the little bamboo coffee table. The windows were wide open, letting in the sunlight.

'Thanks, Ahmed,' she said, as they passed in the doorway.

The houseboy gave her a happy smile.

'Welcome home, Sister,' he said.

She went through the sitting-room into her bedroom and peeled off her clothes. They had had an early start that morning, leaving the volcanic basin shrouded in mist, and there had been no time to wash herself in the uncomfortable outhouse round the back of the cabin, even if she could have forced herself to face the ordeal of cold water under a hand-held shower.

Now, as she stepped into her tiny bathroom, she was ready for all the pampering that she could get. . .warm water, perfumed soap, bath oil, fluffy towels. . .the whole works! Even the most sophisticated health farm couldn't improve on what she was planning!

She emerged an hour later feeling like a princess. Wrapping herself in her freshly laundered sarong, she sat down on a bamboo chair beside the window, gazing out at the lush vegetation of the tropical garden. A couple of large brightly coloured birds were perched in the palm tree near her window, conversing with each other in strange, exotic, musical sounds.

She remained by the window for several minutes, simply soaking up the peace and beauty and trying to restore her sense of equilibrium. As soon as she felt completely rested she planned to go across to Obstetrics and see baby Deborah again.

As she thought about her precious little patient she felt a pang of sadness for that other premature baby who hadn't survived. Chris's baby had only lived three months. No wonder he was extra careful about letting premature babies go home before they were really developed enough! She could understand him being cautious. As for Deborah, she was barely a month old. It would be weeks before she was fit to leave.

Sara stood up and went across to the tiny cupboard that served as a wardrobe, deciding that she would put on her uniform even though she wasn't on duty. It would look more appropriate if she gave Deborah her feeding bottle.

Even as she reached for the clean white dress hanging in the cupboard she heard someone calling her name.

Ahmed was running up the stairs. 'Dr Stephens is asking for you, Sister. You are to go to the surgical house.'

She buckled up her silver belt and pinned on her cap, hurrying down the stairs.

Chris met her at the door of the surgical unit. 'There's been a road crash,' he began tersely. 'I need to operate at once if we're to save this man's life.' He lowered his voice into an urgent whisper. 'Sister Poleng has had very little experience of surgery. You're the most senior sister, and the most experienced in surgery. I'd like you to scrub up, stat!'

There was no time to ask questions if a man's life was at stake.

As she moved inside the cool air-conditioned theatre, Sara could see why it was the pride and joy of the clinic. So rarely used, the equipment was brand new. Sara found herself wondering why the road crash victim had come to them. Wouldn't he have been better off at the Rumah Sakit, the public hospital in Denpasar?

She voiced her thoughts briefly as she scrubbed up beside Chris in the tiny ante-room beside the theatre.

'You haven't seen our patient,' he told her in a tense voice. 'I doubt if he'd survive the journey to Denpasar.'

She followed Chris into the theatre, where a hurriedly assembled team of their most experienced nurses was waiting. Sara felt a wave of trepidation sweeping over her. Her theatre experience had all been in the same hospital in London with surgeons who had been with her throughout her training. And the nursing staff had been friends and colleagues she knew well. But these faces behind the masks belonged to nurses she barely knew. Some were from an entirely different culture from her. How would they all react as a team under the stress of a full-scale operation?

But as she looked down at the patient lying still beneath the dressing sheet she forgot her fears in her concern for this gravely ill man. Speed was of the essence if he was to live.

Chris was making a careful examination of the patient's injured legs, which had obviously been badly crushed in the accident.

'The left leg is viable,' he said evenly, 'but I'm afraid I'll have to amputate the right one.'

A muted gasp of dismay ran around the little theatre. Chris's eyes above his mask were troubled. He raised his head and addressed himself to the team, in a firm but decidely husky voice.

'Let me tell you something about our patient. His name is Mr Ketut Wirawan. I've spoken with his wife, who survived the crash relatively unharmed. She understands the seriousness of her husband's injuries and has given me permission to perform whatever surgery is necessary to save her husband's life.' He lowered his voice. 'If any of our junior staff would prefer to leave would they do so now?'

No one moved. There was silence in the theatre, broken only by the whirring of the air-conditioning.

Sara looked at Chris as he waited. She saw the deeply concerned expression in his eyes and wondered how she could have ever doubted his integrity. Here was a man who was totally committed to preserving life and improving the health of his patients.

As their eyes met, Chris seemed to relax.

'Scalpel, Sister.'

Sara was fully in control of her nerves as she handed Chris the instrument for the first incision. It was as if she were back in London again. She had received a good training at St Celine's and had plenty of practice in theatre. An amputation was a sad operation. No one liked to have to remove a limb, but if it would save the man's life they had no alternative. She had to be objective about the situation and set an example to the less experienced nurses.

Dr Astuti was acting as anaesthetist, and Chris constantly checked on the patient's condition as his expert fingers worked on the badly injured limb.

At one point it seemed to Sara that they might lose the patient. Chris called a halt while he applied cardiac massage, and there were a few tense minutes before he deemed it safe to continue the operation.

Sara handed over the sterile sutures and helped him

to sew up the stump. It was only as she applied the bandage at the end of the operation that she had time to ask him for details of their patient.

'How old is he?' she asked.

'I don't know,' he replied. 'I would estimate in his forties. His wife was too upset to answer questions. I got her permission for the amputation so that I could act as quickly as possible. There's a driving licence somewhere, but I hadn't time to inspect it. The police have it.'

A male nurse arrived from the pathology unit with the results of the grouping and cross-matching. Until then; they had been giving only plasma to their patient.

'Group O-negative,' said Chris, pulling off his mask and running a hand through his damp hair. 'Would you see to the IV, Sister, and stay with the patient until I've spoken to his wife again and dealt with the police?'

After a short period in the small but well equipped recovery-room, Sara accompanied her patient to one of the larger rooms in the surgical unit. Two nurses had been assigned to help her, and she set about explaining to them how to special the patient. It appeared that the surgical unit was equipped with the latest technology for monitoring her patient, but she had to be sure the nursing staff knew how to operate it.

Chris returned as she was adjusting the IV.

'I've sent off to Denpasar for some more blood,' he told her. 'And I've got some more details of our patient. His name, as I told you earlier, is Ketut Wirawan. He's forty-five and comes from Penelokan near Batur, and he's a farmer. His wife was too distressed to tell me anything else. I've given her a sedative, and she's sleeping now in the medical unit.'

'Poor woman! Any idea why they crashed?' Sara asked.

'The police say Mr Wirawan was trying to overtake on that narrow bend just half a mile down the road from here. A motor-cyclist was coming the other way, and our patient apparently swerved to avoid him and ended up in the ditch.'

'But is his wife uninjured?' she asked.

Chris nodded. 'She's been very lucky. Her husband took the weight of the car on his legs when he was crushed beneath it. But Mrs Wirawan, strapped into the passenger seat, escaped with minor cuts and bruises. Sister Poleng admitted her because she was understandably suffering from shock. And now the added distress of realising her husband has lost a limb. . .Would you go along and have a few words with her later in the day when she comes round from the sedative I gave her? You may be able to comfort her. I think it's too early to explain that her husband will walk again with a prosthesis. Simply listen to her and be sympathetic.'

'Of course.'

Sara turned back to her patient, fixing sandbags at either side of the stump before erecting a bed cradle over the top. Chris helped her to fix everything in position before she turned her attention once more to the IV.

'Are you still glad to be back?' he asked her.

She gave a gentle smile. 'Of course. How about you?'

'I'm glad we were here when Mr Wirawan was admitted.'

'So am I,' she agreed.

His eyes lingered on her face. 'Look, I'll get Sister Poleng to take over for a couple of hours this evening. Would you like to have supper with me. . .maybe at home?'

Her heart began to pound. It was the seductive way he pronounced the word 'home'. Even in the middle of changing an IV she could still feel sensually aroused if Chris was around. And the look in his eyes said that he felt the same way. All the pent-up frustration they had both been feeling out at Batur had to be released some time.

'Sounds good to me,' she said quietly.

She stayed with her patient for the rest of the day, but as the twilight fell Sister Poleng arrived to take over.

'I'm here until Night Sister comes on duty,' she told Sara. 'So go off and enjoy yourself.'

'I'm not leaving the compound tonight,' Sara said. 'I'll be on hand if you need me.'

She hurried over to the obstetrics unit and spent half an hour with baby Deborah. The nurse on duty was happy to hand over the feeding bottle to her. Even in the three days of her absence Sara could see a marked improvement, and the baby's weight had gone up too.

Finally she went along to the medical unit to speak to Mrs Wirawan, the wife of her amputation patient. She was relieved to find her more composed than she had expected. The effect of a few hours' sedated sleep had helped to calm the unfortunate Balinese wife.

Mrs Wirawan's English was good; Sara could tell that she was a well-educated lady. There was very little more she could do for her except listen. The nursing staff on the medical unit had apparently been very kind. She was anxious to see her husband, but didn't want to disturb him until he was fully round from the operation. Sara suggested that the following morning would be a good time.

'My husband is a very important man in our community,' Mrs Wirawan told her, without a trace of pride. She was merely stating a fact, giving Sara a little more background information about her patient. 'He will not take kindly to being bedridden. It may take some time for him. . .to come to terms with what has happened to him.'

'Don't worry,' Sara said gently. 'We shall be very patient with him. But for the moment, concentrate on getting your own strength back. Rest again, and if there's anything you need, the nursing staff will get it for you.'

The dark, expressive face creased into a sad smile. 'You are all very kind. Thank you very much for all your help.'

Satisfied that all was well, Sara went back to her room to prepare for the evening. As she went into her room she heard Chris's voice down in the garden.

'Bring your bikini down to the pool for a swim,' he called. 'I'll meet you there.'

She looked out of the window in time to see him disappearing down the ravine path that led towards the swimming pool. In the half-light she could barely distinguish what he was wearing, but the flash of a white towel disappeared into the trees.

It was almost dark, but she remembered the swimming pool had lights all around it. She tossed her uniform on to the bed and stepped into her bikini, winding her sarong over the top of it and slinging a towel around her shoulders.

The path from the house to the swimming pool was steep and stony. She stumbled a couple of times and steadied herself against a palm tree. There was silence all around her except for the croaking of the frogs. She was surrounded by trees that appeared tall, forbidding shapes in the dim light. It was as if she was in the middle of the jungle.

Keeping her eyes steadily fixed on the bright lights of the swimming pool, she hurried through the trees. Chris was swimming towards the side of the pool as she emerged from the darkness. He waved his hand.

Sara threw her sarong and towel on to one of the sun-loungers and dived into the deep end, striking out towards Chris with firm strokes. It felt so good to be in the water again!

He was swimming towards her; as he came close he put out a hand and touched her bare shoulder.

'Thanks for assisting me today,' he said, his eyes searching her face. 'I know I told you to take the day off after your ordeal in Batur. I don't know what I'd do without you, Sara.'

She heard the dry huskiness of his voice as she trod water.

'I'm sure you'd cope,' she said, finding his blatant

admiration almost too much to take. Was this real, no-strings-attached admiration?

Looking at the tender expression on his face, she decided it had to be.

She moved away from his tantalising grasp, dispelling the sensuous urges that threatened to claim her when she was near to him. Time to swim! Keep moving!

They were swimming side by side along the middle of the pool. Chris set the pace and Sara was able to keep up with him. But even as she raced along she was aware of the nearness of his body, aware that he only had to reach out his hand and she would shiver with sensual excitement.

After several energetic lengths he called a halt by the deep end.

'That's enough! You'll wear yourself out,' he called, playfully splashing water on to her face as she touched the bar.

'I could go on all night,' she laughed, splashing him back. 'Let's keep going. . .'

'No!' He put out his hands and took hold of her bare shoulders, his fingers gently caressing her skin. 'Be still for a moment and listen to the fascinating music of the night. The tropical birds and insects are tuning up their nocturnal symphony orchestra ready to entertain us until the dawn arrives.'

Sara remained motionless, feeling the warm water lapping around her body, aware of the tantalising sensation of Chris's fingers moving slowly over her. It was the first time she had ever wanted to make love in the water, but the feeling was almost irresistible. She felt like a mermaid being wooed by the king of the sea.

And the exotic orchestration of the nocturnal creatures around them only added to the illusion.

When he drew her into his arms, she didn't resist. His lips were hard, passionate, demanding and all-consuming. There were no problems, no inconsistencies, no suspicions, nothing but total harmony, sensual excitement and love. . .wonderful love. . .

CHAPTER TWELVE

THE feeling of unreality continued throughout the following morning. Sara found it difficult to concentrate on her work. She had to forcibly hold her mind on the task she was doing so that she didn't start remembering the ecstasy of their lovemaking.

When she saw Chris walking down towards her on the surgical unit she felt herself going literally weak at the knees.

'Good morning, Sister,' he said, in a provocatively languid voice, his eyes raking over her starched white uniform dress and coming to rest on her face.

She was in the process of explaining to a junior Indonesian nurse how to check Mr Wirawan's blood pressure. The girl's attention had strayed to watch the handsome doctor, and Sara knew she would have to continue the lesson later. By herself she could cope with her feelings for Chris, but not with a junior watching her avidly.

'Carry on with your other duties, Nurse,' she said. 'I want to consult Dr Stephens about something.'

Chris smiled. 'Do you have a problem, Sister?'

She longed to tell him that she hadn't recovered from their passionate idyll, that she was even more hopelessly in love than ever before. But she merely smiled as she assembled her professional thoughts.

'Mr Wirawan is still asleep, but he's been fully round.

I've spoken to him this morning, and as soon as he's awake I'll let you know.'

'Yes, please do that,' he said. 'I want to answer all his questions and let him know what's happening. Have you seen his wife today?'

Sara nodded. 'She's a remarkable woman—a very strong character, I would say. Sister Poleng is going to bring her along to see her husband later this morning.'

'Good.'

She was so terribly aware of how close he was to her. His white coat was almost brushing her bare arm. How long did sensuous feelings like these take to wear off? She had never experienced anything like it. It was as if she were still possessed by this man. She wondered what he was thinking as he looked down at her, that strange, enigmatic smile on his sensuous lips. . .those lips that had driven her wild only hours ago. . .

'I've asked Staff Nurse Williams to take over here for a few hours today,' he said. 'I'd like you to help me out with the Holiday Camp.'

She watched his face breaking out into a huge grin.

'You mean the tourists who squander their money on treatment they don't need.'

'Exactly!' he said. 'We need to prune out the ones who are only here for the luxury pampering. They'll have to find themselves a health farm—I need to keep some spare beds for my sick patients.'

'But I thought you liked the revenue they brought in,' Sara began.

'Up to a point,' he said carefully. 'But there are absolutely too many of them now. If we had a real emergency I wouldn't have enough beds. So, we'll go along and persuade a few of them to depart.'

'You know, there's one thing that puzzles me,' she told him. 'The difference between the standard of treatment here and the standard of treatment up at Batur. Those poor patients in that dismal cabin have so little. Why is that?'

His eyes flickered dangerously and she realised she'd overstepped the mark again.

'Sara, I wish you'd stick to nursing and leave the administration to me,' he said, with studied calm. 'As I've told you, there are some things I can't. . .or don't choose to. . .explain to you. This was one reason why I didn't want to take you to Batur. But you insisted on prying into my affairs, and. . .'

'I wasn't prying!'

She took a deep breath to calm herself, realising that in raising her voice she had attracted the attention of the other staff in the surgical unit.

She looked down at her patient, who was stirring uneasily in his sleep. He opened his eyes and reached out his hand in a weak gesture.

'Water. . .give me a drink.'

Sara leaned across and reached for the feeding cup on her patient's bedside locker. She realised that she was trembling with indignation. . .and furious with herself for breaking the rapport between them. It had taken so long to gain Chris's confidence, and with a few inquisitive words she had shattered everything.

'I'll see you along in the tourist unit,' said Chris, his voice cool and professional.

She heard him striding away from her as she helped

her patient take a drink. Mr Wirawan sank back against his pillows, murmuring a barely audible 'Thank you,' before drifting back into sleep.

Time enough to bring her patient up to date with what was happening. Let him remain ignorant for as long as possible.

A couple of hours later, relieved of her post-operative nursing duties by Staff Nurse Vanessa Williams, Sara went across to the tourist unit.

This time when she encountered Chris her feelings were tempered with annoyance that he should still be holding out on her. In spite of their passionate idyll of the night before, in spite of all the love and tenderness he had shown her, he still could not bring himself to confide totally in her. What was he hiding? Why did he need to be so secretive?

She thought all secrets had been brought out into the open after her stay at the Batur clinic, but apparently Chris thought otherwise. It wasn't going to be easy to cope with this conflict of emotion. On the one hand she was hopelessly in love, on the other she felt her trust and confidence in Chris being eroded, being tested to the limit. . .and she didn't think she could go through all that again, even for someone like Chris.

She found him in his consulting-room on the ground floor of the tourist unit. As she went in she decided the room looked more like the manager's office at a luxury hotel. Holiday camp wasn't the right description. The people who paid through the nose to be pampered were highly sophisticated and usually well off—they had to be if they were able to pay the fees Chris demanded!

Chris looked up from the patient he was talking to and smiled at Sara as if nothing had happened to shatter her illusions.

'I'd like to examine Mr Taylor, Sister. Would you show him into a cubicle and give him a dressing-gown and slippers?'

Sara did as she was told. As she handed out the regulation white fluffy towelling dressing-gown and slippers she couldn't help thinking it was all a bit over the top! Why on earth these pampered patients needed such European luxuries in the heart of the tropics where temperatures were soaring into the nineties, especially when her poor patients at the Batur clinic. . .

She gave herself a mental shake. Time to stop musing about Chris's administration. She would only go round in circles and finish up by distrusting him completely.

Chris came into the cubicle and did a thorough examination. Sara, presiding over the examination trolley, anticipated her chief's requirements and handed over the instruments without him having to voice a request. At the end of the proceedings, Chris pronounced their patient fit and advised him that he was well enough to leave and continue his holiday.

In answer to the expected request, Chris explained that he was extremely sorry, but it wouldn't be possible to prolong his stay. . .no, not even for a higher fee. The patient's bed was unfortunately required. Yes, it had been a pleasure to treat him. And if further medical problems arose the patient would find the Rumah Sakit in Denpasar most agreeable.

Sara couldn't help smiling to herself as the patient took his leave.

'Well, I'm glad you've regained your sense of humour,' Chris told her.

'You're such a hypocrite!' she exclaimed, before she could stop herself.

'No, I'm a diplomat,' he corrected smoothly. 'And one of these days you may realise why I have to be.'

She remained quiet. Best not to stir up the hornets' nest twice in one day.

There was the sound of raised voices from the reception area on the other side of their door. Sara opened the door to be confronted by a large, prosperous-looking man with Eurasian features. Gold teeth flashed in his sallow face as he gave her a wide smile.

'The name's Craig, James Craig, and I've just been telling your young nurse here that I'm going to be admitted today.'

Sara was aware that Chris had jumped to his feet. She thought he was going to remonstrate at the intrusion, but he was coming forward with outstretched hand.

'How do you do, Mr Craig. I'm Dr Stephens. How can I help you?'

The large man was shaking Chris's hand, stepping leisurely inside the consulting-room and looking around him expansively.

'Nice place you've got here, Stephens. I think I'll check in at once. Have somebody bring my bags from the car.'

He tossed a car key across at the nurse who was manning the reception area.

'Sir, I think I should explain, Mr Craig has no

appointment to see you, sir. He's not booked to come here; in fact. . .'

'That's OK, Nurse. Go and get Mr Craig's bag,' ordered Chris. 'Now, do sit down and tell me about yourself.'

Sara stifled a gasp of annoyance. It was one rule for the rich and another for the poor where Chris was concerned! The prospect of a handsome fee was obviously overruling his sense of ethics.

James Craig sat down on the leather chair in front of Chris's desk and leaned forward.

'I've succumbed to the dreaded Delhi belly, or whatever they call it round here. Fact is, Doc, I need a complete rest to get over it. I've had it for days while I've been travelling, and it's not getting any better.'

Chris nodded sympathetically. 'I'll give you a thorough examination and we'll do some tests, Mr Craig. Where have you travelled from?'

James Craig waved an arm expansively in the air. 'From Hong Kong originally. But I've been everywhere. This is a little holiday I planned—Bali's such a beautiful place. Get me better, Doc, and I'll be very grateful.'

I'm sure! Sara thought as she stood behind this self-admitted patient.

'Sister will check you into one of our superior rooms and then I'll come along and get started on your tests,' Chris told him. 'But first a few preliminary questions so I can write up your case notes. Your address in Hong Kong?'

His pen was poised over a clean sheet of paper.

'Oh, just put Hong Kong. I've got several houses

there. I was born there. My father was English; mother was Chinese. . . Look, do we need to go into all this now? I'm finding it hard to sit still, if you know what I mean. . .'

Sara leaned forward. 'I'll settle you into your room and Dr Stephens will finish this later.'

She saw the impatient look on Chris's face. He seemed more concerned about finding out the patient's background than treating him.

'One of the superior rooms, you said, I believe?' She faced Chris over the desk.

He nodded. 'I'll be along in a few minutes.'

As she settled her new patient into the best room in the tourist unit Sara tried to rid herself of her irritation towards Chris. Why was he so anxious to admit this man without even examining him? Was it the prospect of a fat fee, or was it something more sinister? She didn't know what it could be, but she intended to find out.

Chris arrived as she was turning down the sheet, waiting for her patient to come out of his en-suite bathroom.

'We only have his word that he's suffering,' she said shortly. 'He looks pretty fit to me.'

'Just go along with it. . .even if it is a charade,' Chris whispered. 'Give him anything he wants. . .but keep him here—and, Sara, be careful.'

She frowned. 'It's almost as if you've been expecting him to come.'

'I have.'

James Craig emerged from the bathroom dressed in a huge silk dressing-gown.

'Look, just skip the tests, Doc. Give me something for the diarrhoea.'

Chris smiled. 'We'll postpone the tests for a while. I'll give you some Lomotil tablets and we'll see how you get on with that. Meanwhile, feel free to use all our facilities, Mr Craig.'

Sara sat out on her veranda sipping a gin and tonic. She found she needed something to calm her down from the antagonistic feelings she had for Chris. He was sitting opposite her across the bamboo table sipping whisky. The sounds of the night were all around them, but tonight they didn't sound like a romantic symphony to Sara's ears. It was a cacophony that disrupted her thoughts when all she wanted was peace and quiet.

'You're still angry with me for admitting James Craig, aren't you?' Chris said quietly.

She put her glass down on the table, the ice chinking. 'Is it so obvious?'

He smiled indulgently. 'Let's say it stands out a mile.'

'But why did you admit him? I thought we were cutting down on non-emergency patients.'

He took a deep breath. 'Sara, I've said it so often, but please, this time, trust me. I've been wanting to meet this man for a long time.'

She felt a cold chill run down her spine. 'He's involved with drugs, isn't he?'

'You could be right,' he said carefully. 'But I simply want you to carry on with your nursing duties as if he's a normal patient. Leave the rest to me.'

ROMANCE IN BALI 149

She frowned. 'It's so hard to trust you, Chris, when you insist on being so secretive.'

He stretched his hand across the table and took hold of hers. 'One day, my love, I'll tell you everything.'

'Promise?'

'I promise.'

The night seemed suddenly more beautiful, less forbidding. The croak of the frogs was positively musical again. But a little voice at the back of her mind was telling her that she'd enacted this scenario before.

CHAPTER THIRTEEN

For the next three weeks Sara spent a lot of her time nursing Mr Wirawan, her amputation patient. As his wife had predicted, he was a difficult patient, finding it impossible to come to terms with the fact that he was going to need an artificial limb. For the first few days, it was almost as if he expected to wake up and find it had all been a bad dream, that his right leg was still intact and functioning perfectly.

Sara found she had to be very patient with him. She understood what he was going through and knew from experience of similar patients in London that it could take a long time and recovery would be slow.

But one morning at the end of three weeks she found him sitting up in bed with a smile on his face.

'I suppose you couldn't make me a bit taller when you order that new leg for me, Sister?' he said, with a merry twinkle in his eye.

Sara smiled back, relieved that her patient appeared to have come to terms with his condition.

'I'll see what I can do, Mr Wirawan. Is your wife coming in today?' she asked, feeling for the pulse in his wrist.

'Of course. Even though she's gone back to Penelokan she'll make the effort to get down here. She's a very busy lady in the community. So am I. I own a great deal of land up there, so naturally the administration of the area is of paramount importance to me. The sooner I can get back to my committee work, the better. There is much to be done in the Batur area.'

Sara was listening intently now. 'You work on a committee in the Batur area?' she asked.

Her patient nodded. 'I am in charge of preserving our ancient heritage. In these days of mass tourism we have to be careful here in Bali that our beautiful land isn't spoiled. You wouldn't believe the sort of ideas and schemes that are put forward for our approval! As the chairman, I have to be very strict.'

Sara swallowed hard. 'I can imagine.' She reached for the thermometer. 'Just put this under your tongue, Mr Wirawan.'

With the patient silenced she had time to think. Did Chris have any idea who their patient was? Did he know they were caring for one of the pillars of Batur society?

She spent longer than usual with her patient that morning, making sure that he had everything he needed. She changed his sheets, plumped up his pillows and checked that he had enough iced water. Then she rebandaged his stump after applying a sterile dressing.

He joked that he could still feel his right leg and would she scratch his knee for him?

She put down her forceps on to the dressing trolley and smiled. It was so good to see her patient in such excellent spirits. His strength of character was coming out now. When he had been lying miserably ill and wretched after the operation she had had no idea what he was truly like, but now she could see how a man like this would be a commanding presence in his community, how he could sway decisions. If only she could influence him into reconsidering the Batur clinic!

As she walked away, after settling her patient comfortably back on his pillows, she reflected that she was in danger of becoming as devious as Chris.

Her next task was to make a dutiful call on James Craig. He was one of her least favourite patients. In fact, she found it difficult to think of him as a patient at all. In the three weeks since he had admitted himself she had come to dread his syrupy, soft-soapy manner, and she was always glad to escape from his room.

But Chris insisted that she include James Craig in her morning rounds, so she couldn't very well disobey. She had pointed out to Chris that she had discovered the remnants of some Lomotil tablets unsuccessfully flushed down the lavatory in Mr Craig's bathroom. She doubted whether he had ever had diarrhoea in the first place. Certainly the promised tests had never materialised. But Chris had been adamant that they keep him at the Temple Clinic for as long as he wanted to stay . . .and pay!

Sara took a deep breath to rid herself of the unwanted thoughts. The man might be a total impostor, but she had to remain professional about the situation. Maybe some of the money that James Craig parted with would find its way to their patients at the Batur clinic. If she kept that at the back of her mind she would be able to be civil to the man.

'Good morning, Mr Craig,' she said breezily. 'How are you today?'

The Eurasian features creased into a wide smile of

welcome. 'All the better for seeing you, my dear. You're looking stunning as always. Beats me how you do it—always dashing around the place, never a minute to spare.'

'Yes, I'm always busy,' Sara said lightly, as she picked up the thermometer and prepared to go into her morning routine. 'Under the tongue, please.'

She glanced down at James Craig as she went through the motions of taking his pulse. He was wearing yet another pair of silk pyjamas, open at the neck to reveal a large golden medallion. A huge diamond, set in a wide band of gold, adorned his ring finger. The expensive designer watch on his wrist nudged her fingers as she took his pulse. In any other patient she would have removed it to make sure it didn't get in the way, but there was no need to do that here. There was nothing wrong with James Craig, and the sooner Chris kicked him out, the better she would like it!

'Perfect, Mr Craig. You're in excellent health,' she told him, putting the thermometer back in its holder. 'I expect Dr Stephens will be discharging you any day now.'

'When I'm fit, Sister, when I'm fit,' was the reply she had expected. She had heard it so many times before. But the morning charade was always repeated.

He knows he's not fooling me, she thought as she met his eyes. It's a game of cat and mouse. But what's he up to? And what was more to the point, what was Chris up to?

She escaped as soon as was decently possible, walking out into the clinic garden, feeling the sun hot on her face. She had gone on duty early that morning and was definitely in need of a coffee break. She decided she had time to go over to the house. Ahmed made the most delicious coffee; she only had to show her face in the mornings and he would reach for the percolator.

'Nick!' Her eyes lit up as she saw her patient walking towards her along the clinic garden path. He was carrying a duffel bag slung over his shoulder and grinning from ear to ear.

'I've come to torment you for a couple of days,' he said happily. 'Don't worry, Sister, I'm not going to ask for one of your precious beds. I'll sleep under the stars.'

'Of course we'll find you a bed,' said Sara. 'Come along to the house—I was just going to go back for a quick coffee. When did you arrive in Batur?'

'Just now. I got a lift on a lorry going south. I've been wanting to leave for a week now, but Dr Green thought we should be absolutely sure I was strong enough to cope with the outside world.'

They had reached the house, and Sara stepped on to the veranda and turned back to look at her patient.

'And do you feel strong enough?' she asked gently, her eyes scanning his face with professional concern.

Nick smiled. 'I'll take one day at a time. Today I feel great. . .and I'm looking forward to seeing Mai again.'

'Ah, I'd forgotten about your favourite nurse. And I thought I was the one you'd been missing!'

Ahmed, on hearing Sara's voice, had appeared on the verandah. 'Coffee?' he enquired.

'Yes, please, Ahmed, and bring a cup for Nick. . .

and Dr Stephens too,' she added, as she saw Chris appearing through the trees.

'Welcome back, Nick!' said Chris, holding out his hand to grasp their patient. 'Dr Green has been sending me good reports of your progress. Apparently you were very helpful in the group therapy sessions. He must have been sorry to see you leave.'

'Well, I must admit, I was beginning to feel more like staff than patient. It was time to move on,' Nick explained.

'Ever thought of helping out here? We could do with a strong young man like you,' said Chris.

Nick's eyes narrowed, but he looked interested. 'Doing what?'

Chris smiled. 'The job description would be something between porter and trainee male nurse. I need an adaptable person I can trust. You could have a wage . . .to be negotiated, as they say in all the ads. . .'

Both men were smiling now.

'. . .board and lodging and full use of facilities, including swimming pool,' Chris finished.

'Well, now you have got me interested!' said Nick. 'I'm very partial to swimming pools.'

'And the nurses who work near them,' Chris put in lightly. 'How is Mai?'

Nick grinned. 'You tell me, Doctor! I've only just got back here, remember.'

'Well, drink your coffee and then go down to the pool,' Chris said. 'I expect she'll be delighted to see you. I thought she'd been looking a bit peaky lately. Why don't you spend the morning swimming, and then, if you'd like to report to my office this afternoon, we'll work out the details of your job.'

'Thanks a lot!'

Nick drained his cup and began to search inside his duffel bag.

'I brought this for you, Sister.' He pulled out a piece of paper and handed it to her. 'I've started sketching again. I'd like to paint, but there weren't any paints up at Batur. I'll pop into Ubud when I've got time and buy some.'

Sara looked at the sketch in front of her. It was a pencil drawing of the Batur cabin with the mountains, shrouded in mist, forming a mysterious, eerie background. Nick had captured the atmosphere perfectly. She felt a lump rising in her throat as she studied the picture. There was no doubt about it, the young man had talent. And that talent would have gone to waste if she'd left him lying on the sand down at Kuta all those weeks ago. . .

'Thanks, Nick,' she said, her voice hoarse with emotion. 'I look forward to seeing some of your paintings.'

'I'd better give you an advance on wages this afternoon,' Chris said quickly. 'You could go shopping this evening in Ubud—the shops stay open late. I'll check with Sister Poleng to make sure that Mai gets the evening off too.'

Sara watched Nick sprinting off down the stony path to the swimming pool. She put her sketch down on the table and looked across at Chris.

'If I didn't know you better, I'd swear you were

matchmaking, Dr Stephens,' she said, in a pseudo-severe voice.

Chris smiled, a slow steady, heart-stopping smile that sent sensual shivers running down her spine.

'Well, you know what they say; it's love that makes the world go round.'

'Is that what they say?' Sara opened her eyes wide, affecting an air of innocence. 'Seriously, Chris, I'm glad you're giving Nick a job.'

'It will tide him over until he finds out what he wants to do with his life.'

Sara picked up the sketch. 'I think he knows what he wants already. But the trouble is it's difficult to make a living from art.'

'He'll have to compromise—work part-time to keep the wolf from the door and spend his leisure time doing what he really enjoys.'

'Sound advice,' Sara agreed, standing up. 'And now I really should be getting back. I'm on my way to see Deborah.'

'Her parents are coming to see me this evening. I'd like you to be there so that we can give them a full report,' said Chris.

'Of course.'

'And afterwards, we could maybe have a swim...go for a meal...stay at home...?' He had reached out and taken her hand, playfully pulling her down beside him. 'What shall we do this evening, Sara?' he whispered huskily, brushing her cheek lightly with his lips.

'You're incorrigible, Dr Stephens!' she told him, glancing around her as she straightened her cap.

He laughed as he released his disturbing grip on her.

'If you won't give me an answer now, I'll make the decision myself.'

As the sun sank lower in the sky, Sara began to feel the accustomed anticipation of an evening with Chris. As she looked out of the obstetrics unit at the garden bathed in a warm orange glow she remembered the sunsets she had watched with Chris...no, not watched, experienced, because there was more than a visual sensation in the sunsets here on Bali. And with Chris beside her they were even more enthralling.

She gave a big sigh as she looked down at the baby in her arms, sucking away at the feeding bottle. There were so many conflicting facets of her relationship with Chris. But love was the one continual emotion that coloured all her feelings.

'Time you were going off duty, Sister. I can finish feeding Deborah.'

Staff Nurse Williams was standing beside Deborah's cot looking down at Sara.

'Thanks, Staff, but I'd like to finish off myself,' Sara said, with a smile. 'Deborah doesn't like to be disturbed in the middle of a feed.'

'Do you know, I think you really love that baby, don't you, Sister?'

'I know we shouldn't have favourites, but yes, Deborah's very special to me. I'll be sad when she's discharged. I'm going to see her parents this evening. I expect they'll be calling in to look at her before they leave.'

'They seem very laid-back about the situation,' the staff nurse observed. 'They don't visit her very often.

And they don't seem in any hurry to take her away. She's already five and a half pounds. I'd have thought they'd be champing at the bit to get her home.'

'Dr Stephens wouldn't let Deborah be taken away yet,' Sara said quickly. 'He has very strict ideas about prems. Some people may think he's over-cautious, but it's better to be safe than sorry.'

'If you say so, Sister. . .and you know Dr Stephens so much better than I do.' The staff nurse paused, as if weighing up her words. 'I know it's none of my business, but when are you two going to announce that . . .well, I mean, when will congratulations be in order? It's obvious that. . .'

'Nothing is ever obvious,' Sara put in hastily. 'I know medical staff everywhere like to put two and two together, but they often get their sums wrong.'

'But the two of you together seem so ideal. I think it's so romantic!'

The feeding bottle was empty. Baby Deborah gave a final tug on the teat and looked up at Sara as if requesting a refill.

'That's all for now, Debbie,' Sara told her, raising her little patient to an upright position and gently rubbing her back. 'Good girl!' she smiled, at the expected burp. She began busying herself changing the nappy, making it quite clear that she had nothing more to say on the subject of her romance with Chris. Let the clinic staff speculate all they liked! Hospitals the world over were rife with romantic rumours. She would be the first to know if there was anything permanent about her relationship with Chris. But at that moment in time, she felt that the clinic staff probably had about as much idea as she had!

As soon as she had made Deborah comfortable, she checked on her charts, making sure that she knew all the details of her little patient's progress.

Deborah's parents, Fiona and Tim, were waiting for her in Chris's office. Chris was filling them in on the medical details, but he looked relieved when Sara put in an appearance.

'Sister has spent more time with your daughter than I have,' he told them. 'What else would you like to know before you go over to see Deborah?'

The young parents glanced at each other warily. It was the mother who spoke.

'I don't know quite how to put this. . .but the fact is, we were wondering if we could leave Deborah here for a few weeks longer. . .just until she's really strong. You see, Tim's firm have offered him a job in their branch in Singapore. . . I told you he was working in a travel agency, didn't I? It's the chance of a lifetime, but we don't want the responsibility of a premature baby when we're finding somewhere to live and. . .'

'Don't worry, Fiona,' Chris interrupted. 'I wouldn't have let your daughter accompany you anyway—she's far too precious to us! No, I want to make sure she's as strong as a full-term baby before she leaves us.'

The relief the young parents were experiencing was obvious as they turned to look at each other.

'Dr Stephens. . .and Sister Freeman, you've been so kind to us. I don't know how we'll ever repay you,' the young father said earnestly. 'We'll contact you from Singapore and give you an address and phone number.

As soon as we're settled, and as soon as you think Deborah is fit enough to be discharged, I'll fly back to collect her—my firm will give me a subsidised flight on Garuda Airways. I can't thank you enough.'

'It will be thanks enough when we finally hand over Deborah in perfect health,' Chris told him.

Fiona smiled happily. 'We'll go over and say our goodbyes to Deborah. We have to leave tomorrow. I was planning to take her with us if it hadn't been possible for her to stay. I must admit I was so scared about it, but now. . .thanks to you two. . .You know, you two are such a perfect couple. Anyone can see, just by looking at you, that. . .'

There was a broad smile on Chris's face as he interrupted Fiona's display of emotion.

'Anyone can see what?' he asked, faking total ignorance of what she might be hinting at.

The young mother lowered her voice. 'That you two were made for each other. . .and I sincerely hope you've got the sense to see it yourselves.' She broke off, clapping a hand over her mouth in embarrassment. 'Look at me, shooting my big mouth off! Such a romantic at heart! Tim always says I should think before I speak, and. . .'

Her husband was tugging at her arm, anxious to be off before his wife embarrassed him further.

'Twice in one day,' said Sara, half to herself, when they were finally alone. 'People offering their opinion about what they think might be going on between us. I can't understand why they have to. . .'

'I can,' Chris told her huskily, pulling her into his arms. 'It's obvious to everyone that we're in love—we can't hide it. It's a feeling that's so strong it shows in everything we do together, in our work as well as when we're off duty.'

Sara's heart was beating madly. She had never felt so close to Chris emotionally, not even when they had made love and she had cried out in ecstatic fulfilment. But how long could this feeling last? How long before the doubts crept back?

She had absolutely no hold on Chris. She was trying to trust him in blind faith.

'If only you'd confide in me!' she sighed. 'If only you'd tell me what's troubling you when your eyes take on that faraway look and I know you're worrying. I've shared all my secrets with you.'

'Have you, Sara?' He broke away, his eyes searching her face.

'You know I have!' She felt the tortured anguish of his doubting her.

'I've only your word for it. . .'

'But if we love each other. . .' She stopped. Chris hadn't said he loved her; he'd only said they were in love. There was a subtle difference. She had overstepped the mark again. . .and this time in the most vulnerable part of their relationship.

'We should never take each other for granted,' he told her. 'Yes, I'm holding back from confiding in you completely. I can't have total trust in you yet.'

She turned away. 'I think maybe I'll have an early night. It's been a long day and I'm tired.'

'Sara!'

He called her name as she walked away, but she didn't look back.

CHAPTER FOURTEEN

FOR the next week, Sara was wary of how she treated Chris. It was impossible to avoid him on duty, but in her off-duty she made a point of staying in her apartment. Ahmed would obligingly bring her some supper on a tray and she would sit by the window reading well into the night. Occasionally, when the night sounds were stilled, she could hear Chris down on the veranda, restlessly walking backwards and forwards. She longed to go down, to have him take her in his arms again, but she didn't want to start up the whirlwind of her confused emotions again. She wanted to remain calm so that she wouldn't suffer again, because she knew that every time the question of trust between them was raised she felt hurt.

Their love had to be all or nothing as far as she was concerned. She'd had one devious husband, and that was enough for a lifetime.

On duty she was studiously professional with Chris so that he had no cause to find fault with her work. They were polite with each other, but that was as far as it went. Sara realised that they had reached a point at which a decision had to be made; to go on loving, in spite of all the unanswered questions, or to give up and try to regain her emotional independence again.

For the moment she was doing nothing. She couldn't

make a decision when her heart was saying one thing and her head another.

At the end of a week of unease between them, Sara was still searching for a solution as she went on duty. The morning sun was warm on her face, raising her spirits, making her feel stronger in spite of the restless night she had spent, tossing and turning.

She made a beeline for Obstetrics. Half an hour feeding and bathing Deborah would set her up for the day.

Afterwards, she weighed her little patient, and was pleased to find that she was now six pounds. She looked well nourished. The skin had lost its pinched look, and the blonde hair was thickening and growing out from the scalp. Sara took pride in the fact that it was almost half an inch long!

She felt reluctant to put Deborah back in her cot as she prepared to leave for her next call of duty. James Craig wasn't in any way as beguiling as this little patient!

She found her least favourite patient sitting out on his veranda smoking a large Havana cigar. She reflected that everything about the man was outsize. He was larger than life, and seemed to enjoy the caricature he portrayed.

She was surprised to see Nick sitting down on one of the bamboo veranda chairs deep in conversation with Mr Craig. Since taking up his job at the clinic, Nick had done a variety of tasks, but Sara wasn't aware that Chris had given her erstwhile patient any work in Craig's area.

'Good morning, gentlemen,' she said, as she stepped

out on to the veranda. She sat down near the two men, thinking that she might as well join in the conversation. Her nursing duties with Craig would only take a couple of minutes, so she had time to spare. 'What important job are you working on at the moment, Nick?'

The young man jumped hastily to his feet. 'I was just leaving, Sister. I came to deliver the newspaper Mr Craig had ordered.'

'Are you enjoying your work at the clinic?' Sara asked.

Nick nodded. 'It's great. I'm only working part-time—Dr Stephens wanted me to have enough time for my painting.'

'And have you bought your paints yet?'

He smiled happily. 'Oh, yes, I've made a start. I'm working on a portrait of Mai—she's a perfect model. Call in and I'll show you what I've done, Sister. I believe you know which room Dr Stephens has given me, don't you? It's down near the paddy fields.'

Sara nodded. 'Yes, I'd love to see your work. Will you be there this evening?'

'I'll be there from lunchtime,' he told her. 'I'm just working mornings this week, so I've got plenty of time to get on with the painting.'

'I can't get there until after seven, I'm afraid,' Sara said, remembering the full day ahead of her.

'That's OK. Whenever you can make it, Sister.' Nick looked happy and relaxed as he left.

Sara stood up. 'Now, Mr Craig,' she began, 'Let's get our morning routine over with, shall we? If you'd like to put your cigar down we'll make a start. . .'

'Fine young man, that,' James Craig observed expansively. 'I mean, considering his background.'

Sara put her fingers on the pulse at his wrist. 'And what background is that, Mr Craig?'

'I understand he was a drug addict,' he explained in an even tone.

'Who told you that?' she asked.

James Craig deliberately lifted his smouldering cigar from the ashtray and drew deeply on it before replying.

'He told me himself. He's a most likeable, communicative young man. Shows potential. Should go far.'

Sara took a deep breath. 'Provided he goes in the right direction.'

She moved quickly away from him, unable to conceal her dislike of the man. 'There's no point in my taking your temperature with that cigar in your mouth, so I'll be on my way.'

'Sister!'

She turned and looked him full in the face. 'Was there something else, Mr Craig?'

He seemed as if he was about to speak, but then changed his mind.

'No, I just wanted to say thanks for looking after me. I've enjoyed my stay with you.'

'Are you planning to leave us?' she queried.

He looked surprised. 'Didn't Dr Stephens tell you? I'm leaving today.'

'No, he must have forgotten...but then I haven't seen much of him this week.' She hesitated. 'Where are you off to?'

James Craig's craggy features eased into a grin.

'Wherever the spirit moves me. I love to travel. I've no particular plans.'

'Well, I'll wish you a safe journey to wherever you're going,' she said politely, forcing herself to smile.

She went out into the morning sunshine and hurried across to the reception area.

Sister Poleng looked out through the open door of her office. 'Can I help you, Sister Freeman?' she asked.

'I'm looking for Dr Stephens. Do you know where he is this morning?'

'He's in Outpatients,' Sister Poleng replied, a wry smile on her dark features. 'I thought you of all people would know where he was.'

'Thank you, Sister.'

As Sara hurried away she reflected that these barely veiled innuendoes that the staff were giving her did nothing to ease the confusing situation. She felt as if the eyes of the entire Temple Clinic staff were watching her every move as far as Chris was concerned. And nothing seemed to escape their notice. The clinic grapevine must be positively buzzing with the news that there was an obvious rift between them.

She found Chris doing the morning surgery in the small outpatient department. He looked up from the little boy he was examining.

'Did you want to see me, Sister?'

Sara glanced at the Indonesian staff nurse who was assisting Chris. She didn't want to challenge Chris in front of her.

'I'll come back later. . . I wanted to talk to you in private,' she told him.

'I'm having a coffee break in a couple of minutes.

Wait in my office,' he said, returning his attention to the patient.

Sara hesitated. She had a lot of work to do that morning, but still she had to speak to Chris. She had to find out if he knew that Nick had been talking with Craig.

She waited in Chris's office for a few minutes before he arrived, carrying a pot of coffee and two cups.

'I must say, it's nice to see you again socially,' he said breezily as he poured the coffee. 'I had the distinct impression you were trying to avoid me.'

'This isn't a social call, Chris,' she said, trying to sound calm. She accepted the coffee-cup he handed her and took a sip before continuing. 'I understand that James Craig is leaving us.'

'Yes, that's correct. I thought you'd be delighted.'

'I am, but that's not the point. Did you know Nick has been talking to him?'

'Any reason why he shouldn't?' Chris's eyes met hers in a bland stare.

She felt totally confused. 'I don't know—that's why I'm asking you. Nick has told Craig he used to be a drug addict, and I just thought that. . . Look, I don't know what he's getting himself into. I'd hate to see him suffer a relapse. Supposing Craig is involved with drugs? He's the sort of rich, flashy, obnoxious type who could well be making his money from. . .'

'Sara, there are too many suppositions here. You're worrying yourself unnecessarily. Stick to. . .'

'I know, stick to nursing,' she cut in forcibly. 'But it's impossible not to worry about Nick when he's been my patient for so long. He wouldn't even be alive if we hadn't saved him down on Kuta beach.'

She was breathing heavily and close to tears. Chris got up and came round the desk, putting his hands on her shoulders. At the feel of his fingers against her uniform dress all the pent-up emotion of the last week of enforced separation from Chris broke out and a tear slipped down her cheek.

'I'm sorry, Sara,' Chris said, in a husky voice. 'But please believe me when I tell you that no harm will come to Nick. I've got the situation well under control.'

'What situation?' she asked, looking up at him hopefully. Surely he had to let her in on the secret now, when this ex-patient who meant so much to both of them was involved.

He bent down and kissed her gently on the cheek. 'It's better you don't know, my love.'

'I'm not your love!' she flung at him, her voice rasping between the sobs. 'It's over between us, Chris. A relationship has to be based on mutual trust.'

'Exactly!' he breathed. 'This is what I've been trying to put across to you.'

He pulled himself to his full height. 'I've got to get back to my patients, and I suggest you do the same, Sara.'

She looked up into his eyes, noting the veiled enigmatic expression, devoid of all tenderness. She swallowed hard. There was such an air of finality about the situation.

She turned and walked out of his office, hoping against hope that he would call her back, put his arms around her and tell her it was all a mistake. What did she want to know...he'd been such a fool not to confide in her.

But he let her walk away; she could feel his eyes boring into her, hostile, unfeeling, remote...

As she walked over to the tourist unit to begin her morning ministrations she wondered if she was over reacting. Maybe James Craig was harmless enough. Perhaps he was just a lonely tourist who had more money than sense and enjoyed squandering it on pampering himself.

She remembered that she was going to call on Nick that evening to see his painting. Maybe he would be able to enlighten her about James Craig. Perhaps he would set her mind at rest.

She spent the rest of the day in the tourist unit; she had to dispense medication for the patients with gastric problems caused by the change in diet and take specimens from the ones who weren't reacting to medication. Then there were the inevitable sunburn victims who had underestimated the power of the midday sun.

There was a man with a grumbling appendix waiting to see if an operation was going to be necessary, and a young woman who had just discovered she was pregnant and was suffering excessively from morning sickness. Another patient, a seven-months-pregnant woman with high blood-pressure, couldn't decide whether to go back to England or stay on in the comfort of the clinic and have the baby there. Sara spent a long time counselling her and pointing out the pros and cons of the situation whilst leaving the final decision to her patient.

The sun had set before she managed to get away,

and she decided not to change out of her uniform before she went over to see Nick. She would have a long soak in the bath afterwards and then go straight to bed. She felt exhausted.

She reflected that the time-consuming aspect of working in the tourist unit was that all the patients wanted to chat long after their treatment was finished. But now, as she walked over towards the paddy fields to the little cabin that Chris had given to Nick, she felt a deep sense of satisfaction in her work. Yes, she had achieved all she had set out to do today, and more besides. If only she could sort out her emotional life so simply!

Nick looked up from his easel and smiled as she walked in through the open door. 'Welcome to my humble abode.'

'It may be humble, but it's very cosy,' Sara remarked, sitting down on a bamboo peacock chair near the door, where a cooling breeze was blowing in from the fields. 'And I like the décor.'

Her eyes took in the pretty cotton curtains at the window, the matching cushions and a rug in exactly the same shade of royal blue.

'Do I detect a woman's touch, Nick?'

He laughed, putting down his brush. 'Come and have a look at the picture and see what you think.'

Sara stood in front of the canvas and admired the picture of Mai. The young girl was wearing vividly coloured Indonesian dress, long to the ground and draped over her dark hair.

'It's a beautiful portrait,' she said, overwhelmed by

this evidence of Nick's talent. 'I expect this is the first of many more paintings.'

'I hope so. As I said, I take one day at a time,' Nick told her quietly.

As she turned to look at the earnest young man, a brief recollection of the dishevelled appearance he had once presented came flashing before her mind's eye.

'Never go back, Nick,' she told him in an urgent voice. 'Remember there's always someone to help you if you're tempted.'

His eyes flickered. 'Why do you say that?'

She hesitated. 'I wouldn't like you to be influenced by the wrong type of people.'

There was the sound of footsteps on the path outside, and Sara looked out through the open doorway.

Chris stepped inside the cabin, his eyes focusing on her, still dressed in her uniform.

'You're taking your duties very seriously this evening, Sara. Is this a professional visit? Has Nick asked for your advice?'

As if sensing the tension between them, Nick intervened.

'I invited Sister to see my painting,' the young man explained.

Chris seemed to relax. 'Beautiful, isn't it?' He turned to look at Sara. 'I thought you might need an escort back through the garden. It's very dark tonight—too many clouds. It looks as if we're in for a storm.'

He took her arm and steered her towards the door. She wanted to remonstrate, to say that she'd only just begun talking to Nick, that there were so many questions she wanted to ask. But at the firm touch of Chris's fingers she decided it was too late to start stirring things up again. She'd done enough damage for one day as far as her relationship with Chris was concerned.

A flash of lightning broke out over the trees, illuminating the dark, forbidding sky. There was a loud crash of thunder and then the rain began to fall in huge drops.

They ran together, Chris now holding Sara firmly by the hand as they hurried along the path. Once Sara slipped as the rainwater churned the path into mud, and Chris caught her in his arms, but as soon as she was steadied he released her. There was no tenderness in his action. She felt like a stranger who was being dutifully escorted to her home.

The doors and windows of the house had been firmly closed, but Ahmed, anticipating their arrival, flung open one of the veranda doors and helped them inside. The rainwater from their clothes dripped on to the floor.

'You'd better get into your bath as soon as possible,' Chris advised. 'Goodnight, Sara.'

'I'll come down for some supper afterwards, Ahmed,' Sara said to the houseboy, studiously ignoring Chris. 'Could you make me one of your delicious omelettes?'

'Of course. . .and for you, sir?' Ahmed looked at Chris.

Chris hesitated. 'Why not?'

An hour later, as she joined Chris in the main downstairs room of the house, Sara felt the apprehension building up inside her. But tonight it wasn't a pleasurable experience.

Ahmed's omelettes were delicious as always. Sara was ravenously hungry, realising that she hadn't even had time for lunch that day. But as soon as the meal was finished she announced that she was going to bed.

'Wait a moment, Sara,' said Chris. 'I was talking to Mr Wirawan today and he told me he was chairman of the committee for preserving the ancient heritage of the Batur area. Did you know that?'

She hesitated. 'Yes; I was going to tell you. . .but we haven't been very communicative with each other recently.'

Chris ran a hand in an exasperated movement through his sun-streaked hair, still damp from the shower. 'But that was very important. As soon as you found out you should have told me.'

'I don't know what I should and shouldn't tell you any more!' Sara glanced towards the kitchen, and was relieved to see that Ahmed was no longer there. 'Yes, it crossed my mind that you might want to discuss the Batur clinic with Mr Wirawan, but I didn't think you'd welcome my intervention.'

'I would simply have liked to be informed, that's all. But as for your intervening on my behalf, that's out of the question.'

Sara stood up. 'You've made it perfectly clear that you don't want my help. From now on I'll stick to my nursing duties and leave you to your devious activities. But it's over between us, Chris.'

CHAPTER FIFTEEN

THE storm had abated by morning. Sara felt emotionally numb as she looked out of her window at the vapour rising like a cloud of steam from the verdant undergrowth. The night had seemed endless. She had had no sleep in spite of her weariness. But now, as the sun streamed in through the open window, warming her skin, she resolved not to let the rift with Chris affect her work. As to the future. . .?

She turned back into the room and began hurriedly preparing to go on duty. Whatever the future held she would go it alone. Chris had been a wonderful interlude in her life. He had brought fun, excitement. . .and love. In years to come she would look back and think. . .

She brushed a hand over her damp face. She had to be strong about this. She mustn't weaken and think about what might have been.

She decided to do Mr Wirawan's dressing first on her list that morning. Usually she left him until last because he enjoyed a chat with her and she didn't like hurrying him; he was such a pleasant, well-informed, interesting man to talk to. And always at the back of her mind, she had hoped to be able to broach the subject of the Batur clinic.

But today was the start of her new professionalism. She would do her job as a nursing sister, which was all

Chris required her to do. No more...no less. And she wouldn't even think about any of Chris's scheming.

As she walked into Mr Wirawan's room she found Nick working on the air-conditioning.

'Just a temporary fault, Mr Wirawan,' Nick was saying as he screwed back the cover on the wall-mounted machine. 'Some dust was trapped inside... let's see if it works now.' He pressed the air-conditioning switch and the machine whirred into action.

'I didn't know you were an electrician, Nick,' Sara remarked, as she went up to Mr Wirawan's bed.

Nick's face creased into a happy grin. 'Neither did I until this morning. Mr Wirawan sent for me, and I thought I'd have a go before I called in the electrician. It was just a question of common sense, really.'

Sara looked down at her amputation patient. 'Why did you choose to send for Nick?' she asked.

Mr Wirawan smiled. 'Because he's the most easily available member of your staff. Nick will turn his hand to anything, and nothing is too much trouble. He's helped me out of many a difficult situation, I can tell you. It's not easy trying to move around with only one good leg.'

Sara smiled. 'Thanks, Nick. I hadn't realised how versatile you were.'

Nick looked pleased as he started to leave them. 'I'll go and get on with my other jobs—got a busy morning ahead of me. But feel free to call me in any time, Mr Wirawan.'

'Nice young man,' the patient remarked, as Sara began checking her dressings trolley. 'He tells me he used to be one of your patients. I can't believe he was ever a drug addict.'

Sara put down the pack of sterile gauze and turned to look at her patient. 'Is that what he told you?'

'Oh, yes; he seems proud to admit it because he's made such a perfect recovery.'

She swallowed hard. She mustn't say it. . . Chris would be furious. . .but on the other hand. . .

'Yes, he was one of my patients,' she began carefully. 'I first met Nick when he tried to take his own life. Dr Stephens and I had to resuscitate him. Then after weeks of treatment we decided he was ready to go to our rehabilitation clinic—it's a specialised clinic where patients can undergo detoxification and group therapy. It's the only one of its kind out here, and we're in danger of having to close. That would be such a pity, if young men like Nick weren't given a chance.'

Mr Wirawan was frowning. 'Why are you telling me this, Sister?'

Oh, lord, she'd done it now! Sara took a deep breath. It was impossible to retract her words. She had to go on regardless of the consequences.

'Because our detoxification clinic is in your area, Mr Wirawan, and I know you could influence the authorities into reconsidering their decision.'

The frown on the dark face had deepened. 'You're referring to the illegal clinic in that wild, uncultivated area beyond the lake, aren't you, Sister?'

She nodded. 'The clinic is set well back from the road. No one knows it's there unless they're told about it by word of mouth, and that's the way we intend to keep it. It wouldn't affect the surrounding area. . .and it would continue to meet a crucial need in the fight against drugs.'

Suddenly the frown lifted. 'You can be a very persuasive young woman, Sister! But I like your spirit . . .and I like the results of your work if young Nick is anything to go by. I can't promise anything, but I'll see what I can do.'

'Oh, thank you!' Sara stood in the middle of the room, her hands gripping the edge of the dressings trolley.

'Don't become too excited about it. As I say, I can't promise anything at this stage, but I'll work on it. I'll write a letter to my colleagues today. Would you mind passing me my pen, Sister?'

Sara hurried along to reception as soon as she had finished Mr Wirawan's dressing. She had to see Chris and tell him the news! She didn't care if he was angry with her for intervening. It made no difference any more; she was working for the good of the patients.

Sister Poleng was sitting at her desk when Sara approached to enquire about Chris.

'Oh, didn't the doctor tell you? He had to leave this morning.'

Sara took a deep breath. 'Do you know where he's gone, Sister Poleng?'

'I'm afraid I have no idea. Dr Astuti is in charge until Dr Stephens returns.'

Sara turned away. Until Dr Stephens returns! she thought acidly. That could be any time he chose!

* * *

For the next week, Sara was kept busy at the clinic. There was an influx of tourists with minor ailments, and no one was turned away. She wondered what Chris would say when he returned to pick up the reins. But she told herself she didn't care what he said. He shouldn't have gone away just at this crucial moment when she felt she was getting somewhere in her fight for the Batur clinic.

But she had now got used to Chris's disappearances, his deviousness, his refusal to confide in her. If only she could get used to the dull ache in the pit of her stomach that reminded her constantly how much she still loved him!

At the end of a long day in the tourist unit she called in to see baby Deborah. Her little patient had already been fed and was sleeping peacefully. Sara looked through the baby's charts. Steadily rising weight; all the tests were good and the lungs had matured at last. There was no reason now why Deborah shouldn't be discharged. When Fiona and Tim phoned, Sara would be able to tell them the good news.

She went out into the warm twilight. She had a whole evening in front of her and no one to share it with. She would call in to see Nick, find out how the painting was getting on.

The door to Nick's cabin was firmly shut. Even the windows were closed.

Sara frowned as she hurried down the path to the swimming pool. Now that she had time to think about it, she realised that she hadn't seen Nick all day. She usually saw his cheery face at some point during the mornings when he went about his various tasks.

Nick's girlfriend Mai was finishing off her work by the pool, preparing to go off duty. She looked alarmed when Sara asked where Nick was.

'I've a key to his room,' she said. 'Come with me, Sister.'

Sara found herself praying silently as they went back up the path, through the trees to Nick's little cabin.

Mai opened the door and stood back to allow Sara to enter. She switched on the light and looked around her. The painting area was neat and tidy, the new portrait of Mai taking pride of place. Sara went through into the bedroom. The bed was made. She opened the small cupboard. Nick's spare jeans and a couple of shirts were hanging there. In the corner was his duffel bag.

The young nurse had started to cry. 'He's gone, hasn't he, Sister. Nick's left me!'

'I don't know,' Sara admitted, putting an arm round the girl's distraught shoulders. 'I don't know what any of this means. But it looks as if he means to come back here. He wouldn't leave all his belongings. . .and he especially wouldn't leave his portrait of you, Mai.'

'But why didn't he tell me where he was going?'

Sara gave a deep sigh. Why indeed? She knew exactly what the young girl was going through.

Ten days had passed since Chris had gone away; three days since Nick had vanished into thin air. As Sara went down the stairs and out on to the east-facing veranda she found herself wondering if there could be some connection between the two disappearances.

Ahmed appeared with her breakfast tray as she sat down beside the low bamboo table. His bright smile cheered her, and she smiled back. Every morning since Chris had left they had gone through the same routine. It made her enforced separation bearable.

So much had happened since Chris had been away. Mr Wirawan had been as good as his word. He had not only written to his colleagues, but he had convened an extraordinary committee meeting in his clinic room which had taken place the day before. He had asked Sara to be present, ostensibly to take care of him as a patient, but in reality to plead her case. She had been impressed at the standing Mr Wirawan held in the community. He spoke forcibly about his new conviction regarding the legitimacy of the Batur clinic and the necessity for such a humanitarian service. After Mr Wirawan's forceful speech, his colleagues agreed to reconsider their own ideas. It was only a matter of time and formality now before the Balinese authorities were requested to legalise the Batur drug clinic.

Sara sipped the strong hot coffee and broke into one of the rolls, spreading it with fig jam—Ahmed had made a special batch especially for her. All around her the birds were chirping and singing. It was the sort of morning when she should have been so happy. The project she had been working for had been accepted.

But she found she couldn't shake off her leaden spirits however she tried. Life without Chris seemed empty. She had tried to remain emotionally independent, but the fact was that. . .

The sound of footsteps interrupted her thoughts. They were heavy footsteps, but with a jaunty tread. Oh, please let it be Chris! she prayed silently.

She stood up and walked to the rail of the veranda, leaning over so that she could see up the path.

'So you're looking out for me? That's a good sign.'

Chris's voice sent shivers of excitement flooding through her. Her first reaction was to run down to meet him, but she held herself in check. Nothing had changed between them. The angry words they had exchanged before Chris went away were indelibly printed on her mind.

'I didn't know it would be you,' she said, as he came up on to the veranda. 'I had no idea when you were coming back. . .or if you were coming back at all.'

She knew she was being petty, but it cleared the air. He needn't think he could swan back home after a long absence and expect her to rush into his arms!

He sat down on a chair at the other side of the table and eyed her carefully.

'Welcome home, sir.' Ahmed appeared with another coffee-cup and fresh rolls.

'Thanks, Ahmed.' Chris waited until Ahmed had poured the coffee and gone back into the kitchen before he spoke again.

'So—I hear you've been busy with Mr Wirawan.'

Sara looked up, her eyes wide with apprehension. She couldn't tell from Chris's tone whether he was about to reprimand or congratulate her.

'How did you know?' she asked breathlessly.

He gave her a lazy smile. 'A couple of committee members arrived to look over the Batur clinic. They weren't impressed to see the police arresting a man for drug trafficking.'

'Who were the police arresting?' Sara asked anxiously.

Chris leaned back in his chair. 'We got him at last—James Craig. That's not his real name, of course.'

'James Craig! So he *was* into drugs! But what was he doing at Batur?'

'He walked into our trap. Nick had agreed to go along with the idea and invite him out to Batur. Craig was always on the look-out for impressionable young men who wanted to get rich quick. He would lure them along with an initial small fee, promising them untold rewards if they joined his organisation.'

'His organisation? He sounds pretty big in the drugs world.'

'He'd built himself an empire by getting other people to do all the work. No one could touch him; he stayed on the right side of the law. But his need to recruit more and more hapless drug addicts was his downfall. I'd been warned that he was here in Bali. You remember that man who approached me outside the cave at Goa Gajah? He's one of my ex-drugs patients who passes on useful information about the traffickers. Sooner or later I expected Craig to proposition one of our patients, offering money in return for the sale of his illegal drugs.'

'But why did you think he'd come here?' asked Sara.

'Because I'd made a point of appearing to have a foot in both camps.'

A light was beginning to dawn in Sara's consciousness. 'You certainly achieved that!' she said drily. 'I still don't know whose side you're on. I can't believe that you've achieved the downfall of a man like Craig on your own. Who's behind you, Chris? Who's directing you?'

He took a deep breath before glancing around him. There was no one near. His voice was low and urgent when he spoke. 'I'm part of a world-wide organisation pledged to crack all drug trafficking. We're financed by an international consortium of wealthy businessmen who recognise the danger posed by drugs to the stability of the commercial world. Part of the expenses of my clinics are paid by the consortium. It's a sizeable grant, but I don't handle any of it. The finances of the Batur clinic are entirely separate. If the Batur clinic were to appear prosperous it would alert people like Craig to the fact that it was under surveillance. It has to appear to be struggling financially to make it credible. But it doesn't do the patients any harm to have to do some work. It strengthens them for when they go back into the outside world. . . Now, for obvious reasons, all this has to remain secret. I can trust you to keep this to yourself, can't I, Sara?'

She smiled. 'Say that again, Chris.'

He looked puzzled. 'Say what again? Oh, you mean that I can trust you to. . .'

'You've said it! At last!' She moved swiftly around the table, holding out both her hands towards him. 'If you only knew how I've waited to hear you say those words! I. . .trust. . .you. . .'

He pulled her down into his arms, his lips claiming hers in a long tender kiss.

'I longed to tell you, but I felt the less you knew the

safer you'd be if. . .if anyone like Craig started pumping you for details. I couldn't bear to think that you might come to any harm. I've missed you so much, Sara,' he whispered in a husky voice.

She gave a contented sigh. 'And I've missed you. When you go away and leave me. . .'

'I won't need to leave you ever again,' he said tenderly. 'I've finished my assignment here. My contract in Bali was for four years. Apprehending Craig at the end of my time here was a bonus.'

'But where will you go?' she asked.

His arms tightened around her. 'You mean where will *we* go, don't you? I'm not letting you out of my sight again. Always poking your nose into my affairs. . .'

She pretended to aim a blow at his head, and he laughed as he fended off her hand, drawing her closer into his arms.

'But I haven't told you about my success with Mr Wirawan,' she began excitedly.

'I know already. He sent one of his colleagues to the Batur clinic to tell Nick the good news last night.'

'Was Nick with you when the police took Craig away?'

Chris nodded. 'Nick was the bait.'

Sara shivered. 'I'm glad he came to no harm,' she said.

'He's perfectly fit—I brought him back with me just now. He couldn't wait to go and see Mai. I told you I had the situation under control.'

'I remember,' she said quietly, feeling as if the words he'd said had been a whole lifetime before. 'You know,

I've often wondered if Mike was approached by someone like Craig when he was out here.'

She heard the intake of breath as Chris looked earnestly into her eyes. 'Mike wasn't approached. . . he actively went out seeking trouble. It was only a question of time before he got caught. The authorities were on to him before he left Bali.'

For a long time neither of them spoke. Sara leaned back against Chris, feeling the strength of his arms enveloping her in tenderness.

When she spoke, her voice was barely a whisper. 'I didn't know about Mike's activities here on Bali.'

'I didn't think you did. . .but I had to be sure.'

She felt a weight lifting from her mind. She'd finally rid herself of the past.

'So what now?' she asked. 'Who will do your work out here?'

'Another doctor has been trained to take my place,' he told her. 'Another devil-may-care, foot-in-each-camp medical director will appear on the scene. But that needn't concern us, because we shall be winging our way back to England. You would like us to be married in London, wouldn't you, Sara? I've accepted a surgical post—a mere registrar, but I'll soon work my way into a consultancy, especially with a remarkable nursing sister for a wife.'

'You're very sure of yourself, Dr Stephens. I may have other plans for my life.'

'Then let me try to persuade you. I thought we could stop off in Singapore on the way back for a few days. I hear the newly refurbished Raffles Hotel is fantastic. I'll book a suite for our honeymoon.'

Sara was laughing now with excitement. 'Honeymoon? But we haven't had the wedding yet!'

'Does it matter which way round we do things? You and I don't need to be boringly conventional. We'll have the honeymoon first in Singapore and then the wedding in London.'

'If we're going to Singapore we could take baby Deborah with us. She's fit to travel now, but I'd prefer her to travel with us rather then either of her parents—they're inexperienced with babies. They can take over when we reach Singapore.'

Chris smiled. 'Sure you won't be too sad to hand her over? I know how you love babies. But we can have one of our own.'

'Maybe sooner than you think,' Sara said softly.

His eyes widened. 'You mean. . .you don't mean you. . .?'

'I think it's going to be a water baby. It had the most unusual conception. . .'

'Oh, darling!' Chris clasped her so closely she thought she was going to stop breathing. 'So you were holding out on me after all!'

'Only until my secret became obvious,' she whispered.

'No more secrets,' Chris said tenderly. 'Just you and I. . .and our little mermaid.'

'It might be a boy.'

'We'll have one of each. . .when we get around to it!'

Love is in the Air...

Mills & Boon have commissioned four of your favourite authors to write four tender romances.

Guaranteed love and excitement for St. Valentine's Day

A BRILLIANT DISGUISE	-	Rosalie Ash
FLOATING ON AIR	-	Angela Devine
THE PROPOSAL	-	Betty Neels
VIOLETS ARE BLUE	-	Jennifer Taylor

Available from January 1993   PRICE £3.9

Mills & Boon

Available from Boots, Martins, John Menzies, W.H. Smith, most supermarkets and other paperback stockists. Also available from Mills & Boon Reader Service, PO Box 236, Thornton Road, Croydon, Surrey CR9 3RU.

Mills & Boon

Discover the thrill of 4 Exciting Medical Romances – FREE

BOOKS FOR YOU

In the exciting world of modern medicine, the emotions of true love have an added drama. Now you can experience four of these unforgettable romantic tales of passion and heartbreak FREE – and look forward to a regular supply of Mills & Boon Medical Romances delivered direct to your door!

🌹 🌹 🌹

Turn the page for details of 2 extra free gifts, and how to apply.

An Irresistible Offer from Mills & Boon

Here's an offer from Mills & Boon to become a regular reader of Medical Romances. To welcome you, we'd like you to have four books, a cuddly teddy and a special MYSTERY GIFT, all absolutely free and without obligation.

Then, every month you could look forward to receiving 4 more **brand new** Medical Romances for £1.60 each, delivered direct to your door, post and packing free. Plus our newsletter featuring author news, competitions, special offers, and lots more.

This invitation comes with no strings attached. You can cancel or suspend your subscription at any time, and still keep your free books and gifts.

Its so easy. Send no money now. Simply fill in the coupon below and post it at once to -

Mills & Boon Reader Service, FREEPOST, PO Box 236, Croydon, Surrey CR9 9EL

NO STAMP REQUIRED

YES! Please rush me my 4 Free Medical Romances and 2 Free Gifts! Please also reserve me a Reader Service Subscription. If I decide to subscribe, I can look forward to receiving 4 brand new Medical Romances every month for just £6.40, delivered direct to my door. Post and packing is free, and there's a free Mills & Boon Newsletter. If I choose not to subscribe I shall write to you within 10 days - I can keep the books and gifts whatever I decide. I can cancel or suspend my subscription at any time. I am over 18.

EP20D

Name (Mr/Mrs/Ms) _____

Address _____

_____

_____ Postcode _____

Signature _____

The right is reserved to refuse an application and change the terms of this offer. Offer expires 28th February 1993. Readers in Southern Africa write to Book Services International Ltd, P.O. Box 41654, Craighall, Transvaal 2024. Other Overseas and Eire, send for details. You may be mailed with other offers from Mills & Boon and other reputable companies as a result of this application. If you would prefer not to share in this opportunity, please tick box. ☐

Mills & Boon

Four brand new romances from favourite Mills & Boon authors have been specially selected to make your Christmas special.

THE FINAL SURRENDER
Elizabeth Oldfield

SOMETHING IN RETURN
Karen van der Zee

HABIT OF COMMAND
Sophie Weston

CHARADE OF THE HEART
Cathy Williams

Published in November 1992   Price: £6.80

*Available from Boots, Martins, John Menzies, W.H. Smith, most supermarkets and other paperback stockists.
Also available from Mills & Boon Reader Service, PO Box 236, Thornton Road, Croydon, Surrey CR9 3RU.*

Mills & Boon

— MEDICAL ROMANCE —

The books for enjoyment this month are:

PLAYING THE JOKER Caroline Anderson
ROMANCE IN BALI Margaret Barker
SURGEON'S STRATEGY Drusilla Douglas
HEART IN JEOPARDY Patricia Robertson

♥ ♥ ♥ ♥ ♥

Treats in store!

Watch next month for the following absorbing stories:

RAW DEAL Caroline Anderson
A PRIVATE ARRANGEMENT Lilian Darcy
SISTER PENNY'S SECRET Clare Mackay
SURGEON FROM FRANCE Elizabeth Petty

Available from Boots, Martins, John Menzies, W.H. Smith, most supermarkets and other paperback stockists.

Also available from Mills & Boon Reader Service, P.O. Box 236, Thornton Road, Croydon, Surrey CR9 3RU.

Readers in South Africa - write to:
Book Services International Ltd, P.O. Box 41654, Craighall, Transvaal 2024.